IMAGES OF THE DIVINE BIRD

Creating dramatic situations of episodes from her life, her ancestors' histories, or her own imagination, in *Images of the Divine Bird*, Cuban-born American writer Mercedes Cortázar probes the psyche of her characters with irony, clarity, and surgical precision, as well as poetic depth. Sometimes subtle, allusive, metaphorical, and at other times blunt, caustic, and unforgiving, she lets the gamut of human emotions play out in riveting, lapidary prose.

ABOUT THE AUTHOR

MERCEDES CORTÁZAR (Havana, Cuba), recipient of grants including the Cintas Literature Fellowship, edited *Protesta* and *La Nueva Sangre* in New York of the 1960s; was poetry consultant for the translation of *Paradiso* by José Lezama Lima into English (Farrar, Straus & Giroux, 1974; Dalkey Archive Press reprint, 2000); publisher of the digital portal of literature and culture *www.expoescritores.com* (1995-2010); contributor to *Encyclopedia of Spanish in the United States* (Instituto Cervantes and Editorial Santillana, Madrid, 2008). Editor-in-chief and eventually publisher of consumer and business magazines distributed throughout Latin America before her retirement from commercial publishing, Cortázar's literary prose and poetry have appeared in print and electronic literary magazines for nearly six decades. Most recently she contributed an autobiographical essay to *Zilia Sánchez: Soy Isla* (Yale University Press/The Phillips Collection, 2019).

ABOUT THE TRANSLATOR

ANDRÉE CONRAD (Caracas, Venezuela) has translated works by José Donoso, Victoria Ocampo, Robinson Rojas Sanford, and others, as well as Mercedes Cortázar's *Orbs: Collected Poems* (PPI, 2019*)*. As an associate editor at Farrar, Straus & Giroux, she edited Gregory Rabassa's translation of José Lezama Lima's *Paradiso* and other books translated from Spanish, Italian, and Portuguese. Freelancing for several years led her into a long career as a magazine editor.

ALSO BY MERCEDES CORTÁZAR

El largo canto (*The Long Chant*). Havana, Cuba: Editorial El Puente, 1960.

Deux Poèmes de Mercedes Cortázar. French/Spanish bilingual edition. French translation by Servando Sacaluga. New York: Osmar Press, 1965.

Astrogifts. New York: Harper & Row (Harper Colophon Books), 1980.

Orbes 1959-2016: Tierra/Agua/Fuego, Orbe Terrestre, La Afrodita de Cnido, Razón de Eros, Naturaleza en el Espejo. Jesús J. Barquet, editor. Las Cruces, New Mexico: Ediciones La Mirada, 2017.

Orbs: Collected Poems. English translation of *Orbes 1959-2016.* Dade City, Florida: Publishing Partners International, 2019.

MERCEDES CORTÁZAR

IMAGES
OF THE DIVINE BIRD
Autofiction and Stories

Translated by Andrée Conrad and the Author

PPI
PUBLISHING PARTNERS INTERNATIONAL, INCORPORATED
Dade City, Florida
2020

Earlier versions of some of these stories and works of autofiction appeared in the following publications: *Escandalar* (New York), *Mariel* (Miami), *Cucutiar* (Madrid), *TBTN* (San Juan), *Linden Lane Magazine* (Princeton; Miami Lakes), *Baquiana* (Miami), *Signum Nous* (Coral Gables), *El Corno Emplumado* (Mexico City), *Turia* (Teruel, Spain), *The Arabesques Review* (Algeria), and in the International P.E.N. Women Writers Committee (IPWWC)'s *Nuestra Voz/Nôtre Voix/Our Voice: Antología del Comité de Escritoras del P.E.N. Club Internacional*, Volume IV (Salta, Argentina).

Published in the United States of America by Publishing Partners International, Incorporated, P.O. Box 318, Dade City, Florida 33526-0318

Library of Congress Cataloguing-in-Publication Data
A catalog record for this book has been requested.

Printed in the United States of America
First Edition

ISBN: 978-1-7347405-0-9 (pbk)
ISBN: 978-1-7347405-1-6 (ebk)

CONTENTS

●

IMAGES
OF THE DIVINE BIRD

THE FIRST EPIC

1. SHADOW

Shadow comes upon the tiles' intense white, which shimmers with iridescent pinks and blues like mother-of-pearl inside oysters suddenly popping open on the ocean floor. Shadow stretches on down the corridors, sweeping along, first covering, then leaping over obstacles, dusting shaded surfaces with blackness, entrapping a wall. Shadow courses along, ascending a step at a time, its dusky trail linking slits, flattening irregularities. Soon, the wind comes up, cooling those yellow atoms that contract and expand as they shoot skyward, abruptly culminating in an arch rounded at its edges.

Night descends on this structure and, squinting, we seem to discern a stepped temple, an infinite ladder whose mud bricks trap the shadows, along with damp leaves.

Through smoke, we make out lights that assume geometric shapes until a tremor clarifies that these are torches illuminating the night, their white smoke constrained by walls in which stonemasons left square or rectangular openings. Behind the flames we discern the face of the creator god of the universe – Marduk – whose power is ever present, whose golden cloak the moon's southernmost rays give highlights.

Separated by tiny rivers of white plaster, the tesserae of lapis lazuli neatly march behind one another, forming here a wing, there a beard from thousands of clustered circles, each with its own nucleus. Broken up into multitudinous squares, then rebuilt by the illusion that distance creates in our optic nerve, the winged image adheres to the wall, encrusts itself, is subsumed into other walls that ceaselessly multiply.

It's summer, and Marduk's shadow refreshes the thick mosaics that recreate the fantastic life forms of the past, those gardens with hanging leaves and flowers that open their calyxes and spread their petals' heavy, sweet perfume with the coming of night...

Marduk turns on the balls of his feet and raises his hand to point west, the direction towards which torches don't lean and ships never sail.

"I was observing the night through the glass and caught Sirius blinking, a sign as obvious as a door with graceful arabesques carved on it to hide its lock from us," says the god. His metallic mouth gapes wide, pulling the darkness into his throat. Each of the faces contemplating him offers a sign; here, a triangular piece of green jade amazes by hurling rays and swords. Meanwhile, the night dissolves slowly, densely, and, crackling like smoldering magma, pours sleep upon us.

2. MARDUK'S SHADOW WANDERS

Crossing the street, Marduk's shadow destroys sunlight in a shop window, making the glass look like fritted crystal safeguarding ancient alphabets. Marduk? No, those are real shadows, crouching and spying and mingling maliciously, camouflaging themselves in winter solstice's deepest darkness. In the park, the statue lets out a shriek as the birds head south. A rumor that the statue has died spreads through the city.

You wait. What's there to do but wait? Little by little lights come on, knives one by one cutting through the darkness. Here, at the core of the city's fireworks, we contemplate the statue. It's opened its mouth and puts out tiny bubbles with each breath. The sky – why aren't you looking at it? They've cracked its center and its edges are disintegrating, which lets its sap filter into the clouds!

Now, all of a sudden, it's sunny. Up there the brilliance shoots across a sky of incandescent blue. So much light! ...One, two, even three rays smash into manes of lapis lazuli, turning them celestial blue; manes completely drenched in a blue mineral, sapphire shot through with silver.

It's noon, we assume, but what's happened to the birds? In this city – suddenly the birds are all gone and there's just dust?

Walkways mounded with dust, fine sand that seeps through your sandals and sticks to your feet...

What day is today? I ask. You have no idea; you too have lost track. You can't remember, you try to remember, it's futile. Fragments, all fragments, images from this place or that, dreams that end up in the air, like spiral staircases soaring to nowhere in the middle of the desert.

Those manes adorning lions embedded in the walls – so many, so huge! As are the walls themselves, enormous, the color of sand – of course, as that's what they're mostly made of. Or so you tell me – but I know you're lying.

And those tremendous wings, also made of lapis lazuli. You can see the winged bull, the lion with a human face, the man with the head of an eagle. You begin to write on the wall: "When the star appeared in the firmament and the ships lay at anchor many leagues from the city..."

I stop your hand. I can't endure the Sun and the day that have pounced on us, this excessive day swelling around us, devouring us like vultures on a battlefield when evening descends and silence spreads itself over war. I don't want to remember. Our sandals fill with dust and our eyes sting.

We go to the market. It's full of creatures engaging in conversations from other centuries, spoken by mouths that are already dust, in our real-time. They move around, but clearly time clings to the dust. Time does not exist, there is no hurry. And this secret shields the crowd.

There in the distance, in light reflected from the water: the small mountain of stepped stone. It's a witness and the freshness of its shade can be felt, its coolness under the roof. That image reminds us of something: the two rivers that embrace and refresh us. It reminds us of the broken roofs of Nineveh, a little to the north, buried in earth where animals made desperate by the desert's dryness go to graze.

No. We've mixed everything up. Nineveh is still there, its markets flourishing, its gentry strolling around under parasols bedecked with bright foliage and floral motifs… As the morning shines on, the hours are husbanding their untouched reserves to magically transform them at noon, that hour of geometric parity when light and shade divide themselves into equal parts. Then, the Sun's glare will turn into a blinding flash and record us as moving silhouettes for all eternity, our mouths slowly opening in boundless astonishment as the earth, the city, and the torch of Cyrus, its oblivion of smoke, its red flames, its endless black abyss, gradually envelop us.

3. MARDUK'S HERDS

Ill omen: clouds block out the sky in herds, pile up over the mudbrick steps whose bulk shelters us from the wind. Your name is on everyone's lips while gales tear across the flatland.

The stones paving the roadway open their pores to the wind and relinquish their sparse layer of weeds. As the Sun goes down, a light comes up in the observatory. Everyone shudders. "We are all obeying the star's ascendancy," someone remarks.

A smell of torches rarefies the air, projects a violet hue over the roofs of dwellings and the palace walls. A small white assemblage moves forward and everywhere it goes, everyone gives way, making a lane for its vestments to leave a trail in the sand.

Up the temple steps it goes, measuring its stately pace with sacred syllables, sounds dragged out of throats as if they were instruments of great resonance.

Silence. Scents blend, coming from the city as it prepares to eat: aromas from the houses' mud-brick hearths join the odors of burning straw and sand strewn to temper the flames' heat. Spices and incense meld as their chemical makeup transmutes. This lion's mane of smoke hangs in the sky until it unveils the glitter of sharp-pointed stars.

Bejeweled and brilliantly colored garments trailing in the sand, another procession plods over the dunes, and again a crowd shrinks back to let it through. This is the night when the infinitude of nights manifests itself in this unique Night and lets its nectar drip down in footprints, its gradual descent and collapse on the steppes embracing all objects at the same time in a serpentine movement, those flat roofs along with that unbearable white-faced tension of the whole city gazing up at the star's spectacular brilliance. The people lift handfuls of amulets studded with garnets and lapis lazuli to trap the star inside those once-chaotic minerals.

Summer goes on, its heat spreading smoothly over the leaves and lulling the lions that maraud around the city. The suppleness of these beasts confirms their hidden glow as a manifestation of that unbearable light that sits forever at the center of the heavens. A stupor grows inside the walled cities, and those that border on the coast send men in search of seashells that reveal intentions, brain corals whose grooves are roadmaps of the future.

Marduk has not rested all night, and his unceasing work in the temple coats his forehead with sweat and fills his mind with appre-hension. "It's not the star that's hounding me," he says. "It's that cave opening in shadows, the weight of gold on my shoulders, those indelible words carved on the four columns! And look inside the glass – see the egg? Notice how the Sun is making everything clear, how it reaches to the bottom of the oceans where the sea monster curls up? Never mind my corporeal form, that weariness of having to be in perpetual motion, this constant escape and recapture of endless alternatives at a time when everything is happening at once. This weight of gold on my fore-head is the last ray of the star that showed itself tonight, and it won't leave until its will is done."

We study Marduk's golden mouth opening, closing, his crown the legacy of warrior ancestors and the horror he carries in active memory as well as in the depths of his mind.

"Now, should you all choose to look toward the south, you'll see how the ships rest at anchor, how they have left off sailing the skies silently, how they repose. Now we all can rest, after the ancient wars, after those rivers of blood flowed through the city's streets. Visit the observatory, see the prodigy using enormous lenses to scrutinize the universe! Horizon lines have become obsolete! No longer do we need to sketch out plans of cities! Instead, we study the great signs: the movements in the skies, disorders inside our bodies."

Marduk's feet spin in an intricate dance as the segments of the dome open with a metallic sound that rings hollow inside the walls of the temple. The firmament appears, and, at the center of that vibrant black, we can make out the light of another galaxy's suns. Marduk's body picks up the sinister harmony that descends in the form of a light having astral splendor.

Torches, faces bubbling sweat.

Silence.

When Marduk raises his right arm, a stormy sea comes into being. Still attached to the land, this sea is sullied by whimsical creatures that sail across its belly, intermittently squirting jets of water, and by beings phosphorescing in its impenetrably dark depths. Meanwhile, the sky flees in terror, pursued by herds of clouds.

Marduk raises his left arm, ordering fire to appear. The lightning flashes and the flames plunge us all in a scarlet glow.

Lowering his arms into a perfect circle and whirling on his legs, Marduk creates shafts of air that seal all the doors.

4. THE MEASURED PACE OF TIME

Between the two rivers guarding the city, the days creep by on their hands and knees. The feverish activities of the multitudes represent their effort to accelerate time, spur it to a faster pace. The abandoned houses covered again in mosaics no longer reflect those glorious rays of the dying Sun, but instead emit a sickly glimmer, a rancid mist.

Enlil, god of air, flies over the city at day's end, squeezing our hearts with the shadow of his great wings. There, the fate of the world is projected: on his wings we see the mysteries of the past interspersed with the wonders of the future. Those astonishing wings, bizarre images with voices speaking strange languages, unsettle us... Each of us, every person, is represented on one of the divine bird's numberless feathers. Our faces form part of the sacred mosaic, and on each of those hot blue and fiery violet feathers, a whirlwind of images collides until, at last, all this matter lines up in a coherent sequence.

The Sun, a fiery ball whose rays are waves that undulate in surges across the endless solar system, pounces on us. We are weighed down by ancient generations, our remotest beginnings already lost forever in the breeze of time. Shadows of a silent multitude glide over the mosaic walls, on the wings of the divine creature.

The ray passes. The multitude returns to its daily routine: We go back to being I.

"The endless roar of the star," somebody says. "Tonight, the star is growing impatient, producing tremendous reverberations: even its fish are rousing our sea out of its torpor and interrogating it about obscure realities, strange histories of glacial worlds, animals dying as a result of earsplitting sounds inside the earth. Meanwhile, we are silent. We don't know how to be specific and cling to the facts and histories.

"Until the star begins moving west," this sybil continues, "we risk being devoured in fanatical ceremonies that could happen any day now in the city square."

5. TUNNELS AND PASSAGEWAYS

Endless tunnels and corridors, all connected in a frightening matrix of overgrown plants. Atrocious excess of breathtaking objects bisecting our pupils. Acute pain in pleasure. We start to sort out the streets of the city between two rivers, its walls and its fires... Looking in the mirror we see a different city entirely, and instead of griffons, we see gigantic creatures covered in thorns, suns radiating from each pore. We must not look at the inverse image in the mirror or the reflection in a wine glass. We must ignore the cage of fog that's settled over the city.

The sound of a flute crosses the plain. The ageless mountains in the distance welcome the first rays of the Sun, which split on the peaks and multiply in stripes that shoot across the sky. The flute's sound goes on, mingling with the thin haze that's escaped from the desert and is floating over the grass.

Touching the soil produces a damp shock that travels through the senses. Droplets fall on the taller weeds and raise their stalks above the terrain. It's as if everything has begun afresh and this newborn sun isn't going to shine on the alabaster walls and domes of the city, now lost in a pinkish darkness. No, it won't. This solar disc, the four-pointed star giving off rays, this new sun has only appeared over the plain.

All that's left is the sound of the flute in the distance, and here, a mound of grass, a vastness.

And it's not because we want to disguise or hide it, but because we prefer, just for a moment, to get away from the vision of the city. He, too, lifts his eyes from the animals and they wander off in that meaningless vastness, return frolicking, then disappear in their edginess. Gazelles race to plaster themselves on the blue-and-yellow walls, come to a horizontal halt in a segment of time that will endure.

The creature called Enkidu turns his eyes away from those inarticulate animals lacking all artifice, and gets ready to move through veils into civilization, into its dances and inebriation.

"Once you learn the central secret of the body, they won't recognize you. That vibrating, that getting lost in the night as if you had been thrown up by the domes. May the waters of the Sky be contained, and may She not pour Her blood's venom on my shadow!"

This piece of land seems to cause itself to grow, and the idea of covering it with polished stones seizes us, like marking the place where two faces unite and recognize each other. His feet and his hands, his body covered in hair like an animal, his eyes alive with a strange glow…

Under the celestial dome, this unusual encounter, these rivers uniting in their ceremony. She, with her ritual veils, her adornments, her mouth which opens between smiles and exclamations. Above all, her lack of understanding, the vapidness of her glance, tearing her eyes away to look in the opposite direction.

"The animals have all left. All that remains is the horizon. The left portal is closed. All is silent in the cosmic mountain and around our bodies, the waters of the rivers of our ancestors. I have come to reveal to you the fifty names engraved on my body, the roar of our father the abyss, the dance of the winged figures, and the echo of the temple that disappears in the distant city. My body will be named after you, and it will be rebuilt at your command."

Winged creature, your dance and your gaze, your body surrounded by nature, your shadow that comes before you, the secret you reveal to me, the dark penetration of your eyes, your copper body that absorbs the inclement Sun, your lips that spread into a lethal smile, your attributes and veils that float up with the wind, pointing to the distant city you come from, whose light, shadow, rainbow, star, pleasure and repose I know nothing of – what sinister war are you starting in the depths of my body? What thirst are you creating in me? What fire are you spreading?

He who saw the depths and became lost in its spirals, who left his face far away in the distance along with a strange flame rising toward the starry sky, he who transformed the echo into the veins of a leaf, he also has mapped the dark tunnels where we become at once lost and found.

Not you, nothing of you remains, you don't exist anymore, and only my presence rules on that plain. I still blink under the midnight stars. I still hear the murmur of beasts and the transparent silence that descends like a breeze.

And it's not just this, but the mornings, the middays, the interlocking hours on this plain, animals agonizing in traps, the hunter's sharp eyes. And you there, behind the walls, and me here, expanding in this immensity, in these horizons that so quickly recede.

And yet your body is all of this and, under your skin, I can sense the same signals and the same rivers, the same unease and its language. Your scent is a fragrance of both ancient and novel vision, an unforeseen order of things, a sudden encounter with light in a cave's depths.

My life until now, bleak, deprived, drowning in a waveless sea, trapped in its channel without rest. The fifty names lost somewhere beyond the walls, in your body that I do not know, which I dream I have seen and then have lost, which arrives in unconnected parts like promises, like undulations that never end, your body and your tree, your seeds on the earth, your temples and your symbols that drive people mad, your bitter blossoming.

I have never known you because this moment is our own creation, our effort to pluck from night its cluster of circles and intertwine in them and lose ourselves between this lack of understanding and this totality, this sea whose shallowest waters touch the beginning of the abyss, where our bodies' reflections will sleep their eternity.

"No. You know nothing. I bring you knowledge and give these words to you, along with my presence, because they are not your words. They are the ideas of civilization, a world that is not yours and that I bring you in each of my veils, in my movements that suggest truths that you may not yet divine, because your language is not my language, which as yet you don't know. The beast inside you keeps struggling, and what you think you know, you are just dreaming, and I am sketching it for you inside your skull so that you can step into this endless current and float effortlessly as an advanced being, without rushing or worrying. It's not your truth, but mine, not your weariness, but mine.

"And in the future, be careful of your images, lest they open a gaping hole and suck out your mind."

It might seem as if everything is starting anew, and that this newborn sun is not shining on the alabaster walls or domes of the city lost in pinkish fog, and that there is only the sound of the flute in the distance and the expanses of grass … in all that limitlessness.

He stops watching over the animals. They get lost in this insensate immensity, move forward frolicking and then, impatient, disappear. Under the celestial dome, this rare encounter, these rivers that unite in ceremony.

6. CHANGE

My body will be named by you and according to your word it will be rebuilt. You there, behind the walls, and I here expanding in this eternity, on these horizons that spread apart swiftly. Nevertheless, your body is all of this and, under your skin, I can glimpse the same signs and the same rivers, the same unquiet with its own language.

For six days and seven nights I have lived inside your silence. I have learned one by one your rites, your excesses, those limits that no longer restrain you, but which you are determined to challenge. For six days I have survived your splendor. I have immersed myself in your waters, my ardor has answered yours. Now, at this moment, I see the trap coming. I have been created for him. For him, the goddess tenderly worked a fistful of clay, from which came my body, superb but also consoling. Just as you are for me, all your dances created for my contemplation, your words for my ears.

Yesterday, when the moon arose between the branches, you too arose, speaking, reciting incantations, singing your hymns that I know and try to bury. You, too, rose up, and the shadow at the end of your feet became the adjustment of your light.

From the wall they could hear your cries (the echoes reverberate infinitely on the plain).

Your every moment is inscribed in its cracks.

Your rivers are etched on the copper surface that encircles the city.

You for me, all your dances created for me to watch, your words for me to hear. You exhaust me. When, for hours, I watched you arrive (I could see you exploding out of the plain's sounds), I thought: this is the answer, this is the symptom of my mind's madness, this is the secret of my creation.

But now it's over, these useless sensual inventions, this melancholy triggering action. We exhaust ourselves with deeds and interpretations. The animals are running away from me. I'm left alone with my desire, with your words, with ideas descending like mist that wraps around everything, bulks it all out, shrouds pure emptiness with symbols.

What is there for us to begin? The two of us by ourselves in the middle of this plain? Meanwhile, the city must endure an insolent tyrant, and your temple must stand empty without your divinations – everyone destitute.

But this is no time to complain. Let's keep the wheel spinning, and sleep will pour down on us.

"You are a god, Enkidu. Come with me and forget the animals. I'll take you to the city and there you'll meet Gilgamesh, whom no one can equal. You'll see the city that lies behind the walls, maidens and youths as handsome as the stars, arrayed in finery of the most resplendent colors. Why bury your glory out here on the plain, when you can rule and carve your name in the Forest of the Immortals? At this very moment the most powerful king in the world is dreaming about you. In his sleep, he loves you with the devotion of a woman."

7. THE CITY

In the blue city, the one with two rivers, the one with gardens flowing down its steps, the one with four gates, the man-beast roams inside its noise. He makes out faces, in the streets face-paint is everywhere, the day clamors of buying and selling...

There, amidst orchids whose stems disappear inside an obsidian vase, the uncouth face of Enkidu. He's dazzled by the city. Its noise deafens him. The puerile horselaughs and giggles in the streets, beneath the palms, behind the daisy-like parasols... The lassitude of bodies accustomed to plumped pillows, fragrances, decorative facial hair... He can't construct a whole out of this ever-changing mosaic of urban life, its ceaseless activity, its center-of-the-world-ness. All he has is might: the strength to oppose this obscene excess, this prodigal luxury. Enkidu's vitality is his citizenship in this civilization.

And so, he sets out to challenge Gilgamesh. Word spreads in the city that Enkidu dares to defy the Invincible One.

8. THE MEETING

The tyrant Gilgamesh, king of Uruk, was about to exercise his right of first-night. At all weddings he was the first to enter the nuptial bed, then came the husband. On his way to the bride's house, as was the custom, he found the citizens of Uruk lining the street and crowding around outside the house to watch the man-beast, Enkidu, confront their ruler. Spanning the threshold, Enkidu stopped the king from going inside.

The two locked in rage. Roaring like bulls at each other, they smashed the door to the bride's house, the doorjambs shook, the walls broke open, the house collapsed in pieces. Gilgamesh spun, planted his right foot firmly, and hurled the man-beast to the floor. Enkidu lay breathless, vanquished. Seeing Enkidu on the floor panting, Gilgamesh felt his anger fly away. As fury abandoned the most powerful, the other, stunned at his own defeat, exclaimed: "There is no one like you in the world, king of Uruk! The goddess Ninsun who bore you has made you so perfect that you surpass all mortals. Enlil has crowned you, and Marduk has consecrated you, because your force is unique on Earth."

The two embraced, and their fate was sealed.

9. THE LESSON OF EASE

From the mountaintops, Enlil, leader of the gods, has decreed the destiny of Gilgamesh. This comes to the king in a dream that he relates to Enkidu. "The meaning of this dream," says Enkidu, whose gifts include prophesy, "is that the father of the gods has given you your crown, your fate is to rule. Immortality is not your fate. Don't allow your heart to weaken, don't let sadness descend on you! He has favored you with the ability to join and separate, to be both light and shadow to all humanity. He has given you sovereignty over the people, victory in the battle from which no man returns, triumph in sieges and in ambushes from which there seems no escape. Administer that power wisely, treat your people fairly and your palace servants kindly. Be just in the eyes of the old Sun god, Utu."

But after saying this, Enkidu became despondent and went around propping himself up against walls sighing, hiding in corners. Gilgamesh, surprised, asked him, "Friend, why are you heaving these bitter sighs?"

Enkidu answered guardedly: "I've lost all my strength. I'm weak... Worries collide with grief in my throat. Ease and luxury are oppressing and devouring me."

Gilgamesh then became aware that their idleness was sapping him, too. This slothful luxury was not good for them. Thus, the Invincible King's mind turned to the Region of the Living and focused on the Forest of Cedars. There, surely, he would find adventure again.

"I have not yet inscribed my name in stone, as decreed by my destiny. So, I will go to the Region of the Living where the cedars grow. I will carve my name in those trees, alongside the names of heroes of the past and other immortals.

"There, where no mortal man has incised his name, I will raise a monument to the gods. Evil infests that land, so we will destroy it root and stem. There, Humbaba dwells, he whose real name is Enormity. This ferocious giant guards the Forest of the Immortals."

Having met Humbaba while he was roving through the wilderness, Enkidu sighed. "Enlil commanded Humbaba to defend the forest with his life, and armed him with the seven terrors. These terrors seize any living creature who confronts Humbaba. He roars like the torrents of a typhoon, his breath is fire, his jaws are those of Death itself. Why dare to enter that forest and probe its depths? Fear defeats anyone who comes close, because no fight with Humbaba is ever fair, Gilgamesh. The guardian of the forest doesn't even sleep."

"What man can ascend to Heaven?" Gilgamesh replied. "Only the gods live forever with glorious Utu. For us, mere men, our days are numbered, our deeds but gusts of wind. Better to be burned to ashes by the breath of Humbaba than to live the placid life of a woman in the palace."

"My lord, if you are really going to penetrate the Region of the Living, you must inform Utu. Inform the old Sun god Utu, your ancestor: it is his land! The region where the cedars live until they die is the estate of Utu the Abandoned. Inform Utu!"

Gilgamesh gave way to Enkidu's unease. He hunted down a pure-white ram, offered it as a sacrifice to the gods, shook the silver scepter, symbol of his kingship, and spoke these words to celestial Utu: "I would enter the Region of the Living. Be my ally. I would enter the kingdom where the cedar falls. Be my ally."

Divine Utu responded, "So. You are a very great warrior. But who are you to the Region of the Living?"

Gilgamesh answered as a suppliant: "Utu, hear my plea, open your ears to my words, let me come to you, listen to my message. Men in my city die, their hearts oppressed. Humankind perishes, its heart weighed down. I climb to the top of the walls of my city and see their bodies floating in the river. My own end will come like that, I am certain. The tallest man among us cannot reach the sky, he with the greatest stride cannot encompass the earth. I would enter the Region of the Living, carve my name there, and thus live until Enlil soaks these sands with blood and fills this air with poisonous fumes."

Utu accepted the tears of Gilgamesh as the offering of a compassionate man and showed him mercy.

10. The Lesson of Action

Utu, the glorious one, gave Gilgamesh allies – strong allies. He offered him great winds: the north wind, the typhoon, the hurricane and cyclone and tornado. They were like snakes, an army to strike terror, including the destructive blast of lightning. Such were the hosts sent by Utu.

The Invincible rejoiced. He directed his footsteps to the blacksmith's house, and there he forged arms for himself and Enkidu, gigantic pairs of swords and axes, his own "powers from heaven."

Gilgamesh and Enkidu marched off into the black jungles of the plain. They felled trees to make their way, and the children of the city, who wanted to accompany them on the journey, gathered up the fallen timber to carry back home. They trekked up the mountains following them, leaving great bundles of wood to pick up on their return.

On reaching the seventh mountain, the troop abruptly found itself at the edge of the Region of the Living. Without realizing it, they had crossed the threshold and were standing before the mountain with its forest of gigantic green cedars, the house of the gods.

Gilgamesh dug a well within sight of the setting Sun. Pouring libations on the ground, he prayed: "O mountain, abode of the gods, send me a favorable dream!"

They all lay down holding each other close, and sleep poured over them. Gilgamesh dreamed something that brought back to him that they must be vigilant. "My friend," he said to Enkidu, "I've had such a dream of horror and confusion. I was battling a wild bull. The struggle was so fierce that the Sun was blocked by the dust our sweaty and bloody bodies kicked up. I fell to my knees . . . Someone refreshed my forehead with water from a goatskin."

Enkidu said: "Humbaba is no bull, though his form is not ordinary. That wild bull is Utu, your Protector. The moment we're in danger, he'll remove us from the threat. He who refreshed you with water is your guardian god, your ancestor, the third king, Lugulbanda. With his help we'll conquer a fame that will never fade."

Gilgamesh spoke: "After that, I had another dream. We were at the foot of a huge mountain; we were mere flies before its enormity. Suddenly the mountain collapsed upon the plain, trapping my foot under its stones. A blinding glow appeared, and at its center was one whose grace and beauty surpassed all creation. He rescued me from the mountain prison, gave me water to drink, comforted me, set me back on my feet."

"Your dream is auspicious," Enkidu said. "It bodes well. The mountain you saw is Humbaba. Surely, we will kill him and throw his body to the ground, it will fall to the ground, like the mountain that collapsed on the plain."

11. The First Ending of the First Epic

Humbaba, he of the dragons' teeth, he with the lion's face, he of the roar like a torrential deluge, sprang out of his cedar house and waited beside it as the king of Uruk approached. Humbaba fixed his pulverizing gaze, the Eye of Death, on Gilgamesh. Gilgamesh, legs trembling uncontrollably, released a menacing howl. He was afraid for the first time in his life. Unable to contain his tears, Gilgamesh cried out to the heavens: "Glorious Utu, I have followed the route you charted for us, but if you do not help me now, I cannot win!"

Glorious Utu heard his plea and immediately unleashed horrific winds against Humbaba, devastating storms that blinded him and scraped away his protections. The winds scrambled his thoughts with his hair, and threw him down to wallow in the dust.

Humbaba rose up on his monstrous claws, prostrated himself before Gilgamesh, and said: "You who wear the royal garment, prince, delight of the gods, angry bull, resolute in battle, who have made the mother who conceived you delighted with you, who have made the nurse who breast-fed you proud of you: fear not. Let me talk. I've never known a mother. No. Nor has a father raised me. I was born from the mountain. She raised me. And Enlil made me custodian of this forest. Let me go free, Gilgamesh, and I will be your servant, and you my lord. All the trees in the forest I guard will be yours. I will chop them down to build you a palace."

Humbaba took Gilgamesh by the hand and they went inside the monster's house of cedars. The Invincible felt pity. "Oh, Enkidu, isn't it right that the imprisoned bird be allowed to return to its nest? Shouldn't the prisoner be able to go back to the arms of his mother?"

Enkidu replied, "The strongest will be out of luck if he has no judgment. Namtar, adverse destiny, makes no distinction between the living, and will devour him. If this bird returns to its nest, if this captive returns to his mother's arms, then you and I, my friend, will never return to the city where the one who conceived you awaits. This creature will obstruct all roads and make the mountain impassable."

The giant, infuriated, lifted his claws threateningly and released words that echoed up the mountainside: "You servant, you sycophant, you slave who places your feet in the footprints of your master, you contest-loser, you cowardly counselor, you messenger of the royal word, you mirror of others' light! What gives you the right to speak against me like that?"

Enraged and reacting instinctively, Enkidu swung his sword and in one blow chopped off the enormous head that had spewed base insults at him. Then he picked up the head, put it into a sack, and lugged it partway to the boulder where Enlil, intoxicated by his own divine nature, was letting his body soak up the large and small transformations taking place in different parts of the wilderness. Gilgamesh was running behind Enkidu to stop the man-beast, but he was too late: Enkidu bowled the monster's head toward the feet of the god. Sticky with blood, Humbaba's bristly hair coated itself in reddish grit as it rolled through the dirt, and the skull thudded against the boulder. Enlil awoke instantly and leapt to his feet. Appalled at the ghastly sight, the mountain god boomed out portentous blasts of thunder.

"How have you the audacity to set hands on the Keeper of the Forest?" Enlil roared. "To sever his head and hurl his face into the dirt like a war trophy? The Cedar Forest is his home!

"I, Enlil, charged Humbaba with guarding the forest entrances against fools trying to invade the mansion of the gods – this garden lit by crescent moon and star. Now, his great head here? lifeless at my feet?

"For this deed, I cause your days to become night, your food to turn to fire, the water you drink to singe your lips, your faces to be consumed in a long, fraught fight mined with danger and misfortune, and all your struggles in the end to prove fruitless."

IMAGES OF THE DIVINE BIRD

I

Aquamarine and orange: those were the two shades I liked best of the eighteen colored pencils whose wavelengths, I was told, covered the entire visible spectrum, from red to violet, inside the box my mother bought for my first drawing class in elementary school.

The aquamarine of the one pencil began, in my confused senses, with the taste of mint, a flavor that intensified as my eyes saw the bright jangle of yellow and the nostalgic echo of blue mingling to create sea green. After a while, the taste evolved from zesty mint into the sharp sourness of oranges and culminated in a symphonic climax dominated by violas, which tasted of strawberries.

The actual color "orange" I could only imagine from the sadness of the pencil's shell – a brown saturated with red – but then, in that neuter region of wood encasing, there it was, the cylinder of actual pigment, a superabundance of orange so bright it appeared to gyrate in circles, reminding me of saffron dawn's golden glow, reddish tints that domes of mosques throw off as they reflect the dawn.

In those colors I'd suck up the pungent scent of flower buds as their petals opened in fields of jasmine that whiten the horizons, where the melancholy notes of a shepherd's pipe float up, the lonely sound of an invisible flute impregnating the horizon's dull, blue-grey arc.

Orange revealed itself, at my elementary school desk, as a memory of the sea just before nightfall – liquid copper afloat on oily waves, zigzag reflections of masts, rigging, pitch-black bowsprits, menacing booms.

That first encounter with colors awakened a fullness of perception in me: it made all my senses work in unison. Oddly, those perceptions were completely non-verbal. To me, words were mere black letters on a white page: graphic realities. Words had no special meaning: in effect, they were kind of depressing. Words were so insipid that one had to be made to swallow them at that school, which so painfully smelled of ordinary pencils and erasers. I used words, but neither their sounds nor their meanings took up space in my mind. Nonetheless, I thought.

Or rather, I devoted myself to an activity related to what people call thinking.

When this happened, I'd suddenly fall into a bottomless pit. Everything that happened in my daytime life, then, was giving me something to think about. Facts scurried from one place to another, as if they were inside a machine that processed, packaged, and placed lids on them. The furious activity taking place in my head demanded my complete concentration.

It became necessary to transform myself into a completely solitary person so that, free from interruption, I could plunge into that mysterious region so essential to maintaining my mental health. That plane resembled primal chaos, the reality of dreams, where images constantly transformed themselves into others, and voices, resonant echoes like the ones you hear at the mouth of a tunnel, became wise whispers, illuminating murmurs, in which words weren't recognizable, just pure sound.

Sometimes I swam to greater depths in that ocean, and the images as well as the whispers vanished, as if they belonged to the red end of the spectrum and left only their obverse, violet, composed of symbols or concise concepts, axioms and postulates of an esoteric mathematics: like the pure essence that words aspire to reveal but can only reach out to touch.

What I learned in that region had to do with Life and Death, but was so abstract that I couldn't communicate it to anyone. I couldn't even formulate it to myself intelligibly.

II

As I practiced those dives into my own mind, I developed an ability to use words while writing. But the words had taken possession of me, in a very different way from colors and tactile sensations. The outside world stimulated their creation, but they arose from their own particular void. They would fall from the sky and I'd have to write them on a sheet of paper quickly, before they pooled together on the floor like mercury and hid their meanings from me.

Anything I contemplated or remembered might stimulate the coming of words. Among the earliest moments I felt this stimulus was when my mother took me to the psychiatric hospital to visit my uncle.

I had already heard family members talk about him, and the stories they told when we gathered for Easter or New Year's made me intensely curious. What did a crazy person look like? How did he behave? Was a lunatic like a child? How did he talk – what exactly was the meaning of madness?

Years before, my uncle had without warning locked himself in the garage of the big house where most of our family lived. He announced that he needed to dedicate himself entirely to a hugely important project that demanded the utmost concentration. Since my uncle didn't study, or work, or paint, compose or play music, or write prose or even poetry, this project sounded pretty dubious to my family. But, like most things with them, it was the path of least resistance to ignore his odd decision. So they did nothing and continued to dedicate themselves to their customary lassitude, fatigue, headaches, irritability, and other neurasthenic peculiarities.

A week went by before the most dynamic and forceful of my aunts came to visit. Being naturally given to suspicion, she thought it might be wise to investigate what this project was that obsessed my uncle day and night. Being also a woman of action, she pounded on the door from the house to the garage, demanding that my uncle let her in instantly.

When there was no answer, she kicked the door in. She was flabbergasted at what she found.

My uncle, seated at a table covered with a white tablecloth, was carefully tweezing hairs out of his scalp and lining them up, one after the other, in neat rows that by this point nearly covered the table. On placing a hair in a row, he would measure it with a floppy fabric measuring tape and record its length in a notebook.

III

Years later, when I went to visit him at the psychiatric hospital, I tried to discover in his face some trace of that systematic insanity, but his face was normal, peaceful, more like sad and resigned. His long, thin hands had a spiritual quality like those painted by El Greco; moving with nervous gestures, they'd button and unbutton his shirt collar, or repeatedly smooth his thin hair that had begun to turn white. There in the hospital patio, he was sitting on a stone bench, hunched over like Pierrot, lucidly answering all the questions my mother asked. He didn't seem like a child, but neither was he like an adult: he was something halfway between the two. Some of his quick gestures, his crystalline glances, had the spontaneity of a child's, but he also had the solemn demeanor of an adult, burdens weighing down his shoulders, brows frowning in deep concern. My uncle gave me the devastating impression that, years later, I would experience in the theater, at that moment when actors remove their makeup in their dressing rooms and know, at least for that night, it's all over.

That visit to the psychiatric hospital inspired me to write a poem about the freedom of the clouds visible from the sanatorium's cloistered patio. This poem fell into the hands of another of my aunts, very fond of accumulation, and she kept it in her book of mementos, along with sepia photographs of Caruso as Radamès that she'd ripped off the foyer wall of the Tacón Theater as she and the rest of the audience fled when anarchists set off a bomb in the orchestra pit during a gala performance of *Aïda*. In the same album were photos of my aunt's back as she bathed in the erotic manner of Bathsheba, or behind the wheel of her Model T Ford – it's said she was one of the first women to drive a car on the Island – in that golden age when her beauty stopped traffic and shameless men sang to her: "Put your hand here, Macorina!"

IV

In the first years of my life in New York I had a recurring dream: I was at the circus, in Madison Square Garden. After some numbers with trapeze artists in purple tights, toy poodles in tutus doing pirouettes and somersaults, lion tamers in uniforms with gold-fringed epaulettes, clowns in green trousers and jackets with red balls for buttons riding giant unicycles, came the main attraction. The audience fell silent when the lights dimmed and went out. I could hear breathing in the audience as we anxiously waited for the surprise. Suddenly, a blinding circle created by Klieg lights surrounded a fancifully-dressed little Moor (like the black page who runs in to rescue the Marschallin's telltale handkerchief during the last notes of *Der Rosenkavalier*). In one hand he held an object that emitted light and seemed, from a distance, to be a lamp. As he approached my seat, I could see that the Moor was carrying a bird cage – and a small sun was floating inside. Just then the entire audience realized, horrified, that what we were looking at actually was the Sun, shrunken and imprisoned in a cage, and that outside the darkness awaited us forever.

It was at that time I wrote an experimental novel about the appearance of Enlil, Sumerian god of air, in Ur, ancient capital of Chaldea. In my novel, Enlil had manifested in the shape of a huge bird of paradise that, when afternoon came, covered the city's sky, displaying on each of his feathers all events of the past, present and future. Immersing myself in Mesopotamia and Enlil's feathers opened doors to a world in which everything had symbolic weight but was at the same time indecipherable.

One night, coming home from work, I found the door to my room unlocked and the radio blaring the overture to *Semiramide*, Rossini's opera about the legendary queen of Assyria and Babylon, Semiramis. On my bed somebody had left a paper with some trembling and incoherent writing telling me that Merrill Lynch had an interest in my future. The message was followed by a grotesque drawing of a bull's face, symbol of the New York Stock Exchange – but also of the main god of Sumerian mythology, Marduk.

That Saturday I went to the Metropolitan Museum. I avoided the Ancient Near East galleries, with their bas-reliefs of winged lions with human faces from the palace of Ashurbanipal II; the lion in green-glazed terracotta from the door of the temple of Ishtar; and – most especially – the kneeling bull made of silver, its loincloth engraved with geometric designs representing Marduk. I was desperate to avoid the magical communications with which the Mesopotamian world was now tormenting me.

I sprinted to the Impressionist galleries. Whenever I had to flee from the furies, the Impressionists had always welcomed me kindly with their paintings of washed-out landscapes and families enjoying bucolic picnics, captured with imprecise brushstrokes as if the scenes had barely been visible to the myopic painter. Standing out among the Manets, Monets, and Cézannes, there was *Sunflower*, the vibrant creation of a cosmos, the magma of a universe coming to a boil. Its ingenious yellow – which had driven Van Gogh mad – together with its metallic cobalt-blue background, produced the suffering sea-green of its stem and certain areas at its center, and, mixed with red and vermilion, the incendiary orange of its pollen-laden anthers. The cerulean blue in the center, sharp as ice and exhaling an equally antiseptic odor, exhibited a refreshing passivity. The whole painting produced in me the sensation of mint liqueur, derailed in its finish by strident tamarind.

I had contemplated this painting endlessly. During my first months in New York I visited it daily. I was looking for work and my budget only allowed me to eat yogurt on alternate days. Lack of sustenance gave me vertigo, not really unpleasant, but it required me to contemplate Art, and especially that painting, in order to achieve equanimity, perfect spirituality without shame.

Every day I would observe a different facet of that painting, open up a new angle of perception. The painting had come to life, and every day it renewed itself. Like any great work of art, it had extracted the life force from its creator, and now lived nourished by its own sap.

The sunflower expected my visits, and revealed new facets to me with ever-growing enthusiasm, as if it had waited centuries to have a tenacious gaze bring it to life in that artificially lit void of the Impressionist Gallery.

That Saturday, *Sunflower* was waiting for me in the museum, locked in a golden cage decorated in Arabic style with foliage and Kufic characters. On close examination, I could verify that the flower, that roundness bordered with golden petals, had freed itself from its stem and was floating in the sickly pale green and febrile cobalt blue space that Van Gogh had created for it. It depressed me, like visiting a child in an orphanage or an uncle in a psychiatric hospital. The sunflower was spinning frantically inside its cage, and I couldn't free it from the painting where it had been confined.

Suddenly the flower produced a Mesopotamian music that I remembered having heard once on a trip to the Penn Museum in Philadelphia. I had just returned from Europe, and New York was asphyxiating. I got on a bus at Port Authority that went nonstop to Philadelphia, and arrived at the museum at exactly the moment a concert was beginning in the Ancient Near East galleries. On a harp reconstructed from fragments found during the university's excavation at Ur, a Penn professor was playing notes of a funerary hymn deciphered from a cuneiform text. The professor, blue eyes shining behind gold-rimmed spectacles, made the strings of the resurrected instrument vibrate, resuscitating, in sound waves of the living, four-thousand-year-old chords of great melodic and rhythmic complexity based on a pentatonic scale that had remained silent for millennia. All the objects discovered during the excavation of Ur, now resting in the long vitrines of the gallery, began to vibrate to the harp's antediluvian sound. Soon, they were participating in the music's structure as a counterpoint, now delicately, then violently. "It's almost hesychastic in style," exclaimed the professor who'd been playing – British, by his accent. He produced a plastic bull's-head key ring crammed with keys. "Here you have the head of Marduk, but these…these are the keys to the Kingdom!" He opened the center vitrine with one of the keys, carefully replacing the harp on its darker-velvet outline. Then he proceeded to take a few pictures of the harp with a Polaroid camera.

Back at the Met, the sound that the sunflower spinning inside its cage was producing was a kind of whistle, like the music of that harp in the Penn Museum. I looked around and noticed a young woman in a Scottish kilt sitting on a folding chair, copying *Sunflower* using chalk, pencils and a T-square.

"Can you hear the music?" I asked, surprised.

"Oh, yes, isn't it nice? So different from that music one has to listen to in supermarkets. It's as if Americans think music should be processed like cheese, and they give one those orchestral pastiches, with decibels specified by psychologists, experts in obtaining the optimum rhythm for hyper-acquisitiveness." The young woman erased a corner of her sketch with thinly disguised irritation, and began to draw the side of *Sunflower*'s cage, which then became a Gorgon's head.

I swiftly retreated from the Met, at the door colliding with an ancient matron asking a docent, "What're all those lilies doing in

Flemish painting? Lilies here, lilies there, lilies everywhere! What about some tulips?" Outside I saw, barreling down Fifth Avenue past the museum, a bus with a large bull's face on it, and, in Helvetica italics, the slogan "Merrill Lynch Is Bullish on America."

Walking down Fifth towards my seedy hotel, I raised my eyes to the tops of the buildings, eagles' aeries from which thin threads of blood began to trickle, harbingers of the red cascades that would soon spout from the roofs of the skyscrapers and, running down their walls, flood together in the streets with a volcanic roar. I regretted not having brought an umbrella to protect me from those rivers of blood that, from time to time, soaked the city.

While I cowered under a hotel's marquee before the surprised look of a doorman who hadn't noticed the beginning of the crimson rain, I saw, a short distance away in Central Park, three balloons ascend slowly and clumsily into space, and, below, the child who had let go of those helium-filled globes: one sea-green, another orange, and the third yellow. The park was shrouded in a pale mauve mist and the grass was a bouncy, jocular green. I imagined that vast emerald expanse as seen from the opulent terraces of the Fifth Avenue apartment houses: the vegetation, like a jade rectangle, dividing the city into two long rows of megalithic structures, giant dolmens of iron and glass getting lost in the pink of the upper stratosphere, the sound of Ravel's *Pavane pour une infante défunte* resonating on the horizon like supermarket music – like Central Park theme music – the balloons receding, bit by bit losing themselves in the tenderly bluish atmospheric layer that protects us from the deadly effect of gamma rays.

PLASTER OF PARIS FLAMINGOS

Through the window of the bus that runs up Madison, I watched mostly red neon lights flashing on and off, lighting sometimes mannequins, other times fruit vendors' banks of oranges and apples, nestled in blue and dark green squares of cellophane and displayed in startlingly clean, geometric order. Inside the bus, the white fluorescent light turned our faces a cadaverous green. The cold forced people to burrow inside their coats and, when they talked, to expel puffs of steam pregnant with odors from their digestive systems. Taking the bus up Madison on a brutal New York night always elicited something epic and tense in me, like a photo finish at the race track that results in a winning ticket. The fact that nothing ever happened on the bus didn't stop me from harboring those absurd feelings of suspense, or clinging to the parade of silly or dark ideas that assaulted me at night.

I got off the bus and walked the half block to my building. As usual my gaze was monopolized by a Greek vase decorated with the first scene from the *Iliad*, the one in which Athena "moves behind the son of Peleus and yanks his blond mane." Achilles, furious at Agamemnon for co-opting his troops' spoils of war, in effect garnishing their wages, has unsheathed his sword to kill this king-of-kings, but "the goddess with the eyes of an owl" grabs the hero's golden hair with her right hand to stop him from fomenting a revolution; her left hand holds her wonderful shield, witness to a thousand battles, and she does not intend for the Greeks to lose this war just because its greatest hero thinks his troops have been wronged by their bully of a leader. The crudely painted vase is one of those imitations (possibly purchased at one of the Greek shops on Ninth Avenue) of the thousands of genuine Attic vases on display in the Metropolitan Museum and other collections around the world, and replicated in books on classical archaeology. The owner of the hair salon on the ground floor of my apartment, a young Greek immigrant reluctant to abandon his Hellenic past, has made this vase the prime exhibit in his hair salon's window.

This vision every night of the Greek vase made in modern Athens or even in New Jersey, adds itself to the panic and anguish of New York life that mixes things as heterogeneous as the defunct fountain at 59th Street and Fifth Avenue across the street from the restaurant at the Plaza Hotel with its orchestra and harp; those beggars down at Union Square who stand there waving tiny American flags while a man on a soapbox rants about the bloodsucking capitalist economy of the U.S. or the battle of the sexes or the end of the world, in front of the blackened façade of Klein's department store, scene of fierce battles on Friday nights between shoppers who risk deadly upper cuts to the jaw for nylon panties or polyester bras marked down ten per cent. All that jumble of places, objects, people, irritations and images mashed into pulp by the dizzying speed that makes up New York life in a tropical imagination like mine that "never experienced an eighteenth century" but, instead, out of the blue, a Russian Revolution "not red but green as palms" and congealed in supreme horror. That Greek vase in the hair salon of a young American who emigrated from the Piraeus, who lives on stuffed grape leaves from tins opened with a key, and who gives women permanents in a room that has a wall with another badly painted Pallas Athena, now life-size, running with her aegis over her outstretched arm, all rudely drawn by an artist who, like the window's vase painter, did not belong to any school and could not hold a candle to the Berlin Painter, or Euphronios, or Douris, lowly Athenians who made fabulous pottery in the red light district of Athens twenty-five centuries ago.

I quickly climbed the stairs to my room, slammed the door shut, and attacked the typewriter. On the pristine whiteness of the page, the keys typed out, to my surprise, "The Hideous Greek Vase." I had begun to write poetry in English.

Nothing had happened that might have predicted this. I was in good health, my mental state was passable, I hadn't seen any Ingmar Bergman films lately, I hadn't talked to any Cuban exiles replaying "the exile tape" or Puerto Rican intellectuals "the identity tape," or Americans whining about their huge rent and/or their tiny salaries. Nor had I overheard on the bus the eternal conversation about the mysterious, ubiquitous She. ("Do you know what She told me?" "She said... She did... She had to have known everything about it. And then suddenly, She says in this shrill voice...") No, I was going through a normal period. Long past was the one where I didn't answer phones, letters or telegrams. Now, I could answer a call normally, even saying things like "How are you? I'm glad you called. Thank God it's Friday! Have a nice weekend!" I was writing for a women's magazine: articles recasting the psychological problems of American women to be applicable to Hispanic Americans, helpful readings of the occult, etc. My articles had titles like "Meditate to Become Multi-Orgasmic," "The Importance of Jogging for Women with Inferiority Complexes," "10 Easy Steps to Becoming Smarter," "Your Sleeping Pose Reveals Your Fears," "Triumph by Telling Your Mirror: 'Yes, I Can!'" and "Ask the Pyramid!" In other words, I was living a quiet, philistine life amid the maddening megalopolis.

But then the Hideous Greek Vase caught my eye, and what I heard was

WHY DID YOU
ABANDON ME?

It might have been the Spanish language asking me this question in a reproachful tone. But that seemed unfair, given that I had spent so little time in the "Hispanic realm," spoke the language weirdly and with scant respect for the Royal Academy of the

Spanish Language or its august dictionary. I had never chided anyone for saying "*haiga*." I departed the Island too soon to have become a guardian of the language, and in that state of linguistic frailty I had been assaulted by English, which initially I found the funniest language imaginable. As a child, I had learned English along with Spanish but, by some whimsy of my brain, English spoken in the United States was unintelligible to me. People in New York, especially men, seemed to be barking like dogs when they spoke English. I had to renounce that view very quickly if I wanted to stop wandering around the chilly shores of the East River on a stomach emptier than the tin cups of beggars on the sidewalks of Wall Street. This epiphany led to my immersion in the Ocean of English, manifested in tedious repetitions of tape recordings in the language lab at New York University. I learned English but, despite the efforts of distinguished professors of elocution, clung to atrocious accents more reminiscent of the French in Calais than a Cuban of the Vedado neighborhood, where I mainly lived in Havana. Is that snobbery? I don't know.

Writing in English was flouring the pastry top and bottom. I wanted to be able to speak and didn't even try to write in English, except when it was required in college to pass an exam. And that was how culture – knowledge – reached me: in English. I heard in English about the many palaces of the Yellow Emperor, which allowed him to change his residence with the seasons; my path crossed with the lost city of Agade, founded by Sargon; the hairy water people; the Wedel-Jarlsberg, the only family of European nobility whose every member managed to survive the Black Death; the way ladies had their lovers guard the keys to their chastity belts while their husbands were fighting to recover Jerusalem; the predilection of cannibals for French meat; the error of parity theory as it pertains to weak interactions; why Dr. Rudolf Diesel's engine was considered a useless invention for so many years; how Gérard de Nerval would go naked for his nightly stroll in Montmartre, under the light of gas lamps walking his pet crab (which some commentators on Nerval prefer to refer to as a "crustacean," perhaps having in mind a different connotation of the word "crabs") on a string; how the Theory of Mind emerged from studying the language of the chimpanzee Sarah Anne, the first primate (after humans) to communicate "I want my doll." Alas, Sarah Anne died at age 59 on or about August 1, 2019,[1] at home at Chimp Haven, the chimpanzee sanctuary in Keithville, Louisiana, where she had been living in retirement for thirteen years.

Clearly, English was the language to express observations about the entire universe, while the chief purpose of Spanish was to convey neurotic impressions and feelings by minorities like Hispanic Americans, mainly Cubans and Puerto Ricans, or by professors of Spanish who admired the Cuban Revolution or wanted to learn the chachacha. It should be added that Spanish was the language spoken at Victor's Café, where said professors got together with certain progressive American élites and made fools of themselves in the eyes of natives by ordering rice with chicken with black beans.

As an example of Spanish usage, a well-known Cuban-American playwright called one day anxiously asking how to translate *botarse pal solar* into English. I said "street fight," which gives the meaning but by no means conveys the reality. How could English express the vernacular essence of two people engaged in a verbal duel to the death with the entire neighborhood listening in? Seriously, I said after the playwright hung up, must she write about this?

If Spanish is to be used to express the vernacular, and English to communicate all the rest, Spanish then must be akin to the language of schizophrenics, their ways of expressing obsessions and individual, distorted visions of reality. Ergo, Spanish must be the language of literature, especially poetry. Or so I reasoned.

---

[1] Lori Gruen, "The World's Smartest Chimp Has Died," *The New York Times*, August 9, 2019.

Now, when that Greek vase first caught my eye, a kind of spell came over me and I automatically began to write in English. Poetry, a phenomenon inextricably related to the mother tongue, now jumped off the dream train and hooked up with that of meaning. The cultural step signified by hair styling, classical Greek art in the service of hair curling, metamorphosed into the act of writing verse in English, in American/Caribbean English (given its exuberance of metaphors) where the alienation of human beings in great cities could be alluded to. The books I read, cultural programs on television, university lectures, Metropolitan Museum of Art colloquia, took their toll, and instead of singing *La violetera* in the shower, I intoned with an awful accent *Alone again, naturally*.

"*La violetera*" disappeared like Sarita Montiel going down with the *Titanic*, the sequence that gave us Spanish cinematography's cliché of Close-up of Actress's Sad Face > Pan to Fateful Name on Bow of Ship > Sound Effect: Siren Wail That Announces, Like A Modern Sybil, A Sinking in Progress in the North Atlantic. But the violet-selling singer didn't sink with the *Titanic*. She simply lost her voice, and from the debris of the *Titanic* the Apollo spacecraft emerged and flew to the moon.

I had chosen a technical language to express the "tropisms" of my medieval sensibility because

I DO NOT WRITE TO BE
READ BY MY FAMILY.

The fact is, I never, ever wanted to be read by my family. This might be another reason that prompted me to write poems in the language in which I live, rather than the one in which I was born. I've always written as a spy who sends messages to enemy powers, never to show my writings to my family. My psychology is that of the person who puts notes in bottles and throws them into the sea. This caution is rooted in the behavior of my mother: because my other uncle, a poet who co-founded the

Island's communist party, died of tuberculosis, my mother became convinced that writing caused the disease. Every time she caught me writing, she became terrified and would feel my forehead to see if I had a fever and urge me to lie down and rest.

Another possible reason for not keeping in touch with my family is that my vision of my childhood home differs from everybody else's. In my dreams, my house is completely empty, but everywhere I look, there are signs that it's inhabited. The city is very clean and tidy, its houses painted white like those of Mykonos, and everything shines under the shimmering midday Sun. I walk through the empty city and come to my house, and, like the rest of the city's houses, its doors and windows have been left wide open. I walk inside and discover ashtrays with smoke still drifting up from cigarettes, half-eaten fresh avocados, and chunks of *mamey* fruit set out on dessert plates, the vermilion of its succulent flesh contrasting with the shiny whiteness of plates and silver spoons. In my house we never used silver. An intermittent noise like the buzzing of a horsefly comes from my room. I go inside and see the spring wind lifting the white chenille curtains of the panoramic windows in my room, like a sailboat under way, and I have the euphoric, terrifying sensation of participating in a regatta around Cape Horn in bad weather. The buzzing noise is made by a portable fan that moves back and forth, uselessly refreshing the empty room. When a gust completely raises the curtains, the indigo sky seems as pure and cloudless as the desert.

OF COURSE YOU WANT TO KNOW
WHAT HAPPENED TO
THE HIDEOUS GREEK VASE.

The poetic sequence, to use a dull phrase, sprang from the Greek vase and grew by fits and starts. When I started writing it, New York was a blue furnace. The streets radiated an air incandescent, iridescent, even spectral owing to the Sun's intensity, always surprising at a latitude so far north, but that summer it was particularly stifling because the light had to pass through a thick white layer of pollution. The heatwave lashing the city had everybody (except those who could go away) running to buy fans and window air conditioners; the lines at hardware and appliance stores went around the block. Even I, young and healthy, could barely walk across the street before feeling the dizziness that heralds fainting. I arrived at my job the way a forager lost in the Sahara arrives at an oasis, with the anxiety of the asthmatic trying to find oxygen. The air conditioning at the office brought me back to civilization and I could write elegant news items about spontaneous combustion in Ireland (Irish persons were spontaneously catching fire and leaving nothing but their legs, including feet and shoes, in the middle of a pile of ash) and stories of human lightning rods (persons struck by lightning several times in their lives who lived to tell the tale – one of these living lightning rods always kept in his car a pail full of water to put out his hair whenever lightning struck). This fevered journalistic activity would occasionally be interrupted by mysterious hands appearing in a distant window to shake a red-and-white checkered tablecloth: the signal to write a poem in English, with the same subversive attitude that moved Einstein when writing his Theory of Relativity at the patent office in Berne.

The office wasn't the only place I wrote poems in English. In my apartment there was something sacred about the suffocating nights that summer – a calm filled with promise – and after some time, I had enough for a book. I hadn't shown anyone my poems, had no idea what somebody who'd spoken English from the cradle would think of them. Was I writing correctly? Could this work be regarded as poetry in English, from a cultural point of view? Was my management of language and style okay?

I asked myself these questions because I wasn't arrogantly pedantic like some New York Germans, who correct even native English speakers (and, sadly, are usually right). Germans memorize the grammar of other languages by imprinting it on their neurons; what springs from their brains, because they also read what they think deserves to be read in the other language (this is especially true of Germans *vis-a-vis* English literature), is flawless grammatically but abominable phonetically. "Don't ever believe that we will give up being German!" they intimate, knowing that mastery of reading a language gives them the right to speak a language with whatever accent they choose, and in the case of English, which has some roots in German, they remorselessly make it sound like German.

I, by contrast, was full of insecurities about my ineradicable accent though I, too, had made every effort to nail English grammar to my brain with Germanic fury. To me, language is spontaneous, capricious, poetic. I couldn't judge my poems based on my grammar textbook, or manuals for writing poetry in English; those did not provide "perspective." What I needed was this society's most appropriate (yet also most treacherous) resource: the opinion of an expert. I could not show my book to other writers, as I had done in my teens, and ask for their opinion; at my age that would be embarrassing.

I decided to toss these poems along with all their potential grammatical and cultural mistakes into the incinerator. I felt a great lightness in my feet and the cloud that lodged in my brain dispersed. Also, I was overtaken by a corny, semi-Central-European romanticism. I imagined that the Eternal Unknown was out there, wandering the streets, eating in restaurants, sometimes deigning to make emphatic gestures to the faintly audible accompaniment of music by Hollywood composers of the 1940s, pieces like the *Warsaw Concerto* or the soundtrack of *The Best Years of Our Lives*. Under the influence of this style, one icy March morning, I set out to destroy, as Bette Davis would say, "an entirely new batch." With snow seeping through my chapped hazelnut boots and turning them into a white Chinese mountain landscape by Mi-Fei, I searched for a garbage can on a walk down Fifth Avenue and found one in a pocket park between two skyscrapers, those little nooks that take you by surprise with an artificial waterfall flowing down a serpentine staircase of mottled shades of green and pink marble. Into the trash can went the poems with a dramatic "bong." What a moment! I had stripped myself of my work with the same joy that a mummy might experience freeing herself from her shroud.

Happy to erase my name from the Book of Adonai, glad that the Angel of Death would never find a trace of me anywhere, I became intoxicated by my own anonymity and by the assurance that I would continue *ad maiorem Dei gloriam*, as the Jesuits would say. Basically, my attempts to become known had all aborted, either because I attended parties given by Marxist intellectuals (who then constituted the city's elite) in search of being noticed and ended up being accused of causing the Vietnam War, or because I had the habit, peculiar to young persons of the Sixties and Seventies, of insulting consequential people. Of course, being an exiled Island writer in New York was just not cool. The chic thing was to be rich, own a co-op on Park Avenue, and favor communism in "less-developed nations," such as my Island.

But the desperation to emerge from anonymity remained. I even thought to emulate the Surrealists by slashing a famous painting by an Old Master. But every famous painting that came to mind made such an act seem wrong. Descended from Basques on my father's side, I was especially upset when an artist, eventually to become an art dealer for such painters as Basquiat, posed as a Vietnam War protester and spray-painted KILL ALL LIES over Picasso's *Guernica*, then sat down in the middle of the gallery and demanded to see the relevant curator. The vandal was not arrested at the time, nor ever charged. It was just a publicity stunt. *Guernica* now sits in its own pavilion in the Reina Sofía Museum in Madrid, but was then, in 1974, on permanent loan to the Museum of Modern Art, and would continue to be during the lifetime of Generalissimo Franco, who as the autocrat of "neutral" Spain in 1937 had colluded with the German and Italian air forces to destroy this tiny town of Guernica, heart of the Basque country, birthplace of the Basque parliament, site of the sacred tree of the Basque people, and home of the strongest opposition to the Spanish dictator.

Other options for achieving notoriety were also losing their appeal. To ski down the steps of the Empire State Building on roller skates seemed beyond my athletic capabilities, as did transiting the Panama Canal paddling a canoe. The most ambitious stunt I cooked up but never executed, was to forge the signature of David Rockefeller on letters to clients with more than a million dollars on deposit. I was working at Chase Manhattan Bank, of which he was president, had their account information, with names and addresses, and the idea was to notify them to come to the bank at a specific time to close out their accounts because the bank did not want to handle their dirty money. Fortunately, co-workers convinced me that Rockefeller wouldn't think it was funny and I'd be thrown in jail.

Ultimately choosing anonymity over notoriety, I would go to a movie theater after the lights went down and leave before they came back up. I'd give fake names to doctors and dentists, and create imaginary biographies of myself. Sometimes I was born in Algeria, or in the middle of the Atlantic, most often in Latvia or Mauritius. My parents had been Protestant missionaries in Querétaro, circus performers in the Philippines, explorers looking for the source of the Nile in Africa. I was going to be anonymous on purpose, a violet painted on the wallpaper, a zero to the left, the invisible woman, a total nonentity. From that day forward, I would be my own audience. My self-esteem went up or down according to how intelligently or stupidly I chose to be anonymous by means of fictitious identities.

But I just had to write one last book of poems – which I destroyed on the banks of the Hudson River one afternoon. I wore my raincoat like Michèle Morgan's, and as I walked, my boots picked up dry leaves, which made a peculiarly dramatic crackling sound. I imagined that I was walking on the banks of the Seine, studying those Gothic wonders, the spectacular flying buttresses of Notre-Dame; as a fine accompaniment to the scene, Michel Legrand's violins playing *Autumn Leaves* (ah, *Les Feuilles Mortes!*). The poems I carried under my arm were headed for a precipitous marine ending worthy of a Joseph Conrad novel. After several blocks walking at the high speed that used to make people in Havana beg me for visas because they believed I was an American from the Embassy, I stopped to contemplate the panorama. The river bank was crowded with benches occupied by old people, nannies, children playing. Day-laborers and office workers strolled with morose, angelic faces on that idyllic early autumn afternoon. Boats bobbed on the oil-slicked waters, everything greasy and iridescent. I leaned against the railing and looked up at New Jersey on the opposite bank. The sky was covered in clouds as fashionably obese as the Queen of Punt, occasionally broken up by delicate, scattered cirrus plumes that reflected, despite their gauzy transparency, the Sun's fading crimson, all a grand spectacle. The written leaves, my poems in English, exuded the aphrodisiac scent of manuscript paper, and its texture, a little rough under my fingers, gave me the feeling of importance, of destiny. A tugboat sailed down the river, leaving a trail of black smoke, and a train on the opposite bank put out a diminishing wail and a change of tones caused by the Doppler-Fizeau effect. Suddenly I took a sheet of the manuscript and ruined it with one hand, as Napoleon does in movies when a letter displeases him. And, without wanting to see the fate that I had condemned them to, I hurled all the pages to be impaled on Neptune's trident. Afterwards, I saw them drift off like undone white birds, sadly swept away in the polluted current. I let out a philosophical laugh intended to express my mood: Vanity of vanities, all is vanity and vexation of the spirit.

I had become the Hindu trimurti of my own poems: creator, temporary conservator, destructor.

I would persist in this activity until I reached Miami.

HURRAH FOR THE HALF ORANGE,
HURRAH FOR THE WHOLE ORANGE!
VIVA LA MEDIA NARANJA, VIVA LA NARANJA ENTERA
¡QUE VIVA EL COJO CAICÉ QUE VA POR LA CARRETERA!

Miami residents call their city the Big Orange, in imitation of New Yorkers who call their city the Big Apple. Arriving in the Big Orange, now as director of the women's magazine at which I had worked as an editor, I felt like Alice: I'd fallen down a hole, into the looking-glass land of the Cuba of yesterday. I had entered a time machine and strolled through a replica of the intersection of San Rafael and Galiano, where I'd drunk my delicious black *café cubano*, eaten the egg custard called *tocino del cielo* (bacon of the sky as an English-speaking friend called it), and slurped down *mamey* milkshakes. I was rediscovering the delight of tasting tropical fruits as if they were exotic, Cuban food as if it were French *haute cuisine*, spectacularly so at the restaurant called Versailles.

I was just another tourist.

In the Big Orange I continued to create and destroy my poems in English until I ran into an old friend at a party, who convinced me to seek the opinion of the Americans, because what I was doing was committing suicide. She was the voice of reason, I thought. I had to obtain the approval of experts.

I put the poems together in a book I called *Flamencos de losa* in Spanish – Plaster-of-Paris flamingos, the kitschy symbol of Miami that every "serious tourist" brought home to the Island after a shopping trip "up North." My father was one of the multitudes who undertook this daring pilgrimage, returning with a couple of these faux flamingos, which colored my image of the city forever. In my childhood, a trip to Miami was like participating in a Druid ceremony, belonging to a magical cult, having access to the divine emanations of Elohim. Men returned from the North dressed in the latest suit styles, perfectly tailored to their bodies, bought in Miami; the suits gave them an air of self-sufficiency and let them put on that tiny smile of someone who's above it all.

Miami had my whole life been a mythical region: the city of a thousand splendors, ringed by snowy peaks like the Austrian Tyrol, lost in the overpowering clouds of Valhalla.

I had arrived in Miami and instead of mountains I stumbled upon flatlands. The city was a hand-painted tropical tourist postcard, with cobalt-colored sky and clumps of stunning cumulus clouds embracing like the plump women of Rubens, their edges glowing golden in the setting Sun. Everyone here is warm. There's little impetus to compete.

Or so I thought.

MEMORIES ARE MADE OF THIS

On a cinematic night of stark whites and blacks, and a few smudged grays, a woman wrapped in a worn-out raincoat with a twisted belt fastened in a sloping knot weeps in the rain in a forest of trees that glow as if illuminated by the mystical light of the Holy Grail when it appeared to the virtuous warriors of King Arthur's court.

Already in this early sequence of the film, Rainer Werner Fassbinder bids farewell to his life and makes us cry about our own. Another goodbye to life, among the many that Germany has sent us in recent years.

Veronika Voss – film title in English, name of a protagonist, woman in a raincoat: all symbolize a country whose art, literature, and music have always viewed death in a pain-filled, sensual way, and whose pain centers around regret at not having been extinguished with the collapse of its great dream of global domination.

Death and the maiden, eternally interwoven in art, symbolize the orgy of human decay and disintegration that Fassbinder wants to make us experience: a far cry from Aristotle's "noble" tragic catharsis of pity and terror that allows the audience to go home after the performance feeling purged. The director astutely chose his central character, Veronika Voss, closely modeled on a famous actress of the Nazi era who came to be addicted to morphine, to make us experience in an immediate and concrete way death's pitiless, terrifying process of pulverizing and annihilating. Would this have happened, had Fassbinder made the central character a man, following another dictum of Aristotle? "Women and slaves are unsuitable subjects for tragedy, which should rather be kings and noblemen, that is, men not defined by circumstances, but outside of them and impenetrable by them, or at least seemingly so." The protagonist as a woman creates a combination of fragility and vulnerability that intensifies the dramatic tension of the film, and displaces us in the direction of the real-life disaster of our times.

In an apotheosis of the morbid in cinematography, Veronica Voss attends a cocktail party to celebrate her "going away," where she declares that she has entered into conversations with MGM and other Hollywood studios to make films that will lift her career out of its ashes. That elegant, phantasmagoric Art Deco cocktail party foreshadows her own death, soon to take place. Standing next to the grand piano and her accompanist, haloed with spectral backlighting that seems to set her hair on fire, Veronica Voss sings "Memories Are Made of This" in a deep voice. A grotesque scene worthy of the *Satyricon* – and yet devoid of the liveliness and good humor of Petronius or Fellini, alien to the by-comparison-healthy, albeit corrupt, atmosphere of Imperial Rome. In fact, this scene's decadence outdoes even Roman circuses where Christian virgins were thrown to savage beasts, lavish imperial dinners lit by human torches. Veronika Voss' prelude-to-death scene is not offered up as sick "fun" reflecting a perverse tyrant's sadism, but rather as a state of mind, a passion, a philosophy of life. And if it moves us, it is not only because Fassbinder was incubating death in his own body while making the film, not merely because an atmosphere of the Hereafter seems to be infusing the whole; but rather, it shows Veronica Voss as that most powerful of archetypes: a woman-mirror, weak and defenseless, one that forces us to experience our own nightmares through hers.

MEMORIES OF MY LIFE

The memories of Veronica Voss as she sings to all her past and present tormentors arouse memories of my own life. To look back on the past is to parse the etymology of one's own emotional reactions and to confirm the words of Solomon: "There is nothing new under the Sun." Erudition, nothing less than another face of stupidity, is guided by a compass that always points towards one's roots. The question is, why don't we allow ourselves to dream through books? Why not explore the past that this film resurrects for us? – Not the way a student enrolled in a doctoral program prepares an arsenal of facts and theories before the bloody battle of orals or the final thesis defense, but by taking it easy, like Vishnu recumbent on his mighty serpent, whose many heads form a kind of parasol that lets him glide over the infinite waters of the manifest universe. In this mystical journey of the imagination taken with the Hindu god, we can choose here one of the apples of Atalanta, there the poisoned robe of Deianeira. We can sprinkle the eyes of winged Eros with the powder of winged Hypnos. We can filch the Golden Fleece.

In rummaging through the archives of the past, of reality and literature, what else is there brimming with mythological power but that vital antidote to gloom which, sooner or later, breaks into life and manifests itself by means of a cannon blast countering the sound of Life with the gasp of Death, and which expresses, in crippling decibels, the beginning of the end?

THE LIBRARY
OF ALEXANDRIA

One of these journeys of imagination takes me back to the moment when, in the Lyceum library, the unfavorable situation of women first came to my attention. I was a teenager when I sped through those solemn doors with the heartlessness of a hurricane wreaking destruction as it lumbers across the Island. Unaware of the transcendent importance of opening the doors of knowledge, unbowed by burdens or woes, I paid no attention to the trumpets that heralded great events as they blared behind my young back.

The Lyceum was Olympus, and its library the Guardian of Culture, glowing (while emanating a slightly humid odor) on modest shelves curated by benevolent librarians who distributed knowledge with prodigal unrestraint, and who guided my first steps through the catalogues, collections, European literatures, books of medicine, law, physics, metaphysics, mathematics, and psychology.

I visited the library to devour books insatiably. I separated cultures into countries and historical stages, which I later reconnected. I made maps showing, among other events, what was going on in Istanbul while Napoleon was losing the Battle of Waterloo, what was happening in Venice when Abd al-Rahman III named himself first caliph of Cordoba and founded the second Umayyad caliphate. Rejecting my classes at school as superficial, I was resolved to reveal the ramifications and repercussions of all knowledge.

My forceful aunt accompanied me on these pilgrimages to the Lyceum. On my first visit, she had to help me write my name in the registry. Suddenly overcome by my tropical blood's violent reaction to the discovery of Culture, I had found it impossible even to fill out a form. She was Virgil leading me by the hand to explore the heavenly circles (the rings of Hell would come later).

What allowed me to connect my aunt hyperbolically with Virgil in the *Divine Comedy* was that she possessed a mythologically imposing personality that expressed itself, in part, through an obsession with the lineages of Spain's nobility. Sometimes, leaning on the white grand piano in her living room, with light shining through the panes of the balcony door illuminating her hair, my aunt would speak, in her grave, theatrical voice, of our noble dynasties and their splendid feats.

On visiting her house and contemplating those coats of arms and family trees, I made my way through the shadows of time until I reached that golden, operetta-like region where our ancestors performed heroic acts and discovered lands guided by the gallant arm of the King of Spain who pointed toward the Tenebrous Ocean and commanded, *"Hállala!"* ("Find it!"). The command became, quixotically, our own family surname: Ayala. But from those crests also sprouted the faces of my aunt's husband's Villena ancestors, along with their laudable (or dubious) achievements.

Laudable, surely, was Don Juan Manuel, nephew of Alfonso X the Wise, lord, duke, and prince of Villena, author of *Tales of Count*

Lucanor: or, The Fifty Pleasant Stories of Patronio (1335), a collection of moral fables that might have inspired the *Decameron* of Boccaccio – *Tales* was available in copies, but not formally published until 1575 – in plenty of time for the fifth fable, on the treatment of wives, to have been a source for Shakespeare's *The Taming of the Shrew*.

Another de Villena was Diego López Pacheco, who preferred action to words, and was one of three accomplices in the murder of the ill-starred Inés de Castro. This crime provoked the anthropophagic madness of her husband, the Infante Pedro I, eventual king of Portugal. Returning one day in 1355 from hunting, Pedro found his beloved (but morganatic) wife dead, poisoned by "The Three" – López Pacheco along with Pedro Coelho and Álvaro Gonçalves – at the behest of Alfonso IV, the Infante Pedro's father. Pedro made all the courtiers kiss Inés de Castro's exhumed corpse and did not rest until he had devoured the hearts of the two murderers captured, served to him in a silver basin. López Pacheco, seeking absolution from the Pope, had fled to Avignon. After many years, he was pardoned by Pedro, now king, and allowed to return home.

MEMORIES
OF HISTORY

Having learned that some of my aunt's husband's ancestors had written interesting works and had supported artists, but others had poisoned a consort and tried to overthrow the Catholic Monarchs, I was not reassured to find that my own direct ancestors were descendants of a king of Aragon. But let's skip ahead to mere officers and functionaries working for the monarchy of Spain, including, in the seventeenth century, Don Juan Francisco Buenaventura de Ayala Escobar (1635-1727). Born in Cordoba, he crossed the Atlantic to Havana on his own ship. In that most important port of the Spanish empire, he married twice and had children – my ancestors. His titles included Captain of the Army and Navy, and General of Galleons. At some point he was sent to St. Augustine (founded in 1565, the first city in what would eventually become the United States); by 1716 he had been appointed acting governor of Florida, which at that time was a province of Spain. He befriended the Creek Indians; they made him an honorary chieftain; he gave them guns and ammunition to defend themselves against the Cherokee Indians; and that became part of the charges the new permanent governor of Florida accused him of, along with trading in contraband with the British.

So Don Juan Francisco was exiled to Cuba, where he fought to be exonerated of the contraband charge until the day he died. Four years after his death, he was finally cleared of all charges. Thereafter, gentlemen of the Ayala family unremarkably appear as officers in the Spanish royal military ranks. At St. Augustine in 1703, when the British laid siege to the Castillo de San Marcos fort, one Captain Ayala, descendant of Don Juan Francisco, led the Spanish Royal Forces in a sally out to the town square and was shot dead by the British forces commanded by one Colonel Moore. That, and a few other contretemps, ended Spanish rule in Florida.

In 1898, Ayala men helped fight for, and win, the Island's independence from Spain – and participated in the Island's long, fraught relationship with the neighbor to the North.

Exploring for illustrious women in the Ayala family tree was disheartening. The one woman in these lists had all the degrees, diplomas, certificates, and honors of a university professor – and taught in primary school. So, tired of ancestral explorations, I foolishly plunged into the Lyceum's collection of ancients, where "young people in bloom" nurtured themselves on the nectar of History, Literature and Philosophy. The number of discriminatory texts about women was shocking. But I was young – and willing to learn anything interesting.

GREECE
AND ROME

Very like Latin customs of living memory that I for one have cheerfully ignored, Greek society of the Archaic and Classical periods was, for the most part, sexually segregated. All that interesting mythology, and yet well-born young women had little to do with men, before or after marriage. The young woman accepted the husband, often a stranger, chosen by her father. After marriage, she was excluded from matters that occupied most of her husband's time; he was unaware of or feared his wife's sexual appetites. The cultural activities esteemed by the Greeks of the pre-Classical period were, with few exceptions, exclusively male domains: war, politics, art, philosophy, which included math and science. Organized and carried out following well-defined rules, these activities filled the schedules of social institutions, and were the arena in which men could compete with one another and be considered *agathos*, physically superb as well as spiritually virtuous.

LAWS
AND MEDICINE

1. *The Law of the Twelve Tables*, foundation of Roman civil law, enacted in 451-450 B.C.E.:

"Women, young and old, because of their mental lightness, must have a guardian, except vestal virgins."

2. *The Laws*, Plato's unrevised last work, thought to have influenced Roman law, written in the first half of the fourth century B.C.E.:

"Women's natural potential for virtue is inferior to that of men."

3. Plato's *Symposium*, speech of Pausanias, ca. 385-370 B.C.E.:

"I think we haven't yet considered the argument [about love] in quite the right form. We shouldn't be asked to praise Eros indiscriminately. If there were just one kind of Love, then what you say might be true; but since there's more than one kind of Love, we ought to figure out which one should be praised. So I'll begin by saying which Eros is deserving of praise and then try to do it justice by saying why.

"All of us know that Eros is inseparable from Aphrodite. If there were just one Aphrodite, there would be just one Love; but as there are two goddesses, there must be two Loves.

"You might wonder what I mean by asserting that there are two goddesses. The earlier one has no mother, and we call her Aphrodite the heavenly – Aphrodite Ourania – for she is the child of Ouranos. The more recent one is the daughter of Zeus and Dione. We call her Aphrodite Pandemos, or "everybody's Aphrodite," and the Eros who is her co-worker is rightly named common, just as the other Eros is called heavenly. It's important to honor all the gods, they ought all to have praise given to them, but we need to distinguish among their natures.

"Let us now try to distinguish between the natures of the two.

"Now, actions vary according to the manner of their performance. What we're doing right now – drinking, singing, talking – are actions in themselves neither good nor evil. But they become one or the other depending on how you do them. When you do them correctly, they are good, and when you do them wrongly, they are evil. Just so, not every love, but only that which has a good purpose, is noble and worthy of praise. The Eros who is the child of Aphrodite Pandemos is essentially indiscriminate, is what is felt by the meaner sort of men or women or youths, and belongs to the body rather than to the soul. The most foolish of beings are the objects of this Eros, who desires only to gain an end, never thinks how to accomplish the end nobly, and does good and evil indiscriminately. The goddess who is the mother of this Eros is far younger than the other, and born of the union of male god and female goddess, and partakes of both.

"But the offspring of the heavenly Aphrodite, Ourania, is derived from a mother in whose birth no female had a part. The heavenly Aphrodite is from the male god only; her child Eros is that Eros which is of youths, and the goddess, being older, has nothing of wantonness in her. Those who are inspired by this Eros turn to the male, and delight in him who is more valiant and intelligent; it is easy to recognize the pure enthusiasts in the character of their attachments. Their love is not for boys, but rather for intelligent young men whose reason is beginning to develop at about the same time as their beards begin to grow. When they choose a young man to be their companion, they mean to be faithful to him, and pass their whole life in company with him, not to take advantage of his inexperience, or deceive him, or play the fool with him, or run from one to another indiscriminately. Of course, loving young boys should be forbidden, because their future is uncertain. They may turn out good or bad in body or soul, and much noble enthusiasm may be wasted on them. Here, the good are a law unto themselves, while the coarser sort of lovers ought to be restrained by force, just as we try to discourage them from fixing their affections on women of free birth. These sorts of persons give a bad name to Eros, and have led to denying the lawfulness of certain kinds of attachment because impropriety and evil are ascribed to all attachments. But surely, nothing that is decorously and lawfully done can fairly be censured."

4. Marcus Porcius Cato, called Cato the Censor, late third century B.C.E.–first half of second century B.C.E., moralist praised for being the preserver of ancestral custom:

"If a husband surprises his wife committing adultery, he can kill her with impunity, whereas if the husband is the adulterer, the woman cannot put a finger on him because she is prevented by law."

5. Dionysius of Halicarnassus, who emigrated from Asia Minor (modern Turkey) to Rome and wrote in the last quarter of the first century B.C.E.:

"If a woman commits a transgression, according to the laws of Romulus, the injured person becomes her judge and can choose the punishment. The husband and family members judge other offenses, including adultery, or drinking wine. The law determines that both crimes are punishable by death, as they are the most serious crimes that a female person can commit."

6. Livy, *History of Rome*, Year ± 0 C.E.:

"Our ancestors did not want women running businesses, not even private ones, without the direction of a guardian. They wanted women to be under the tutelage of the male members of the family: father, husband, or brother. We (may the gods help us!) allow women to meddle in government and participate in assemblies and the Forum. If women get away with it now, what won't they try later? As soon as they equal men, they will become their superiors."

Livy was the Western World's most influential historian until the 18th century, until, that is, the Age of Enlightenment. His 142 volumes of Roman history emphasize uprightness and morality. To him, the early Romans were paragons of virtue; given this "favoritism," he implied that Roman society in his time (Civil War following the assassination of Caesar through the reign of Augustus) was falling apart before his very eyes. The model of focus and concentration, he's said to have written his histories in his garden in Padua, sending his faithful amanuensis on a donkey all over Italy to buy, borrow, or steal manuscripts of historical interest, then eagerly listening as the slave read them out loud while Livy reclined on a lawn chair, from time to time barking out "Mark that passage!" Then would come days of dreamily organizing his thoughts, followed by dictating feverishly to the amanuensis.

Livy's fretting about women in politics during Rome's Civil War and the rule of Augustus is a clear reflection of the activities of

powerful women. Livia, Julia, Antonia, and other prominent imperial wives, sisters, daughters, daughters-in-law, were a scary lot who
had, if they played their hands carefully, as much strength of will
and power as their fathers, brothers, and husbands.

7. Pliny the Elder, 23 C.E.-79 C.E.:
"A woman was condemned to starve because she had stolen
the key where the wine was kept."

During the eruption of Mount Vesuvius in August 79 that destroyed Pompeii, Herculaneum, Stabiae, and Oplontis, Pliny, fleet
commander of the Roman navy, set off in a fast sailboat followed
by galleys to rescue his friend Rectina, a noblewoman who lived
in Stabiae. The naval vessels docked safely at Stabiae, and Rectina
and her friends boarded Pliny's cutter with baskets full of wine
and food. But when strong winds kept Pliny's vessel pinned in the
harbor and the rain of ash intensified, Rectina disembarked with
her fellow refugees and fled on foot. Pliny knew he was too fat
and asthmatic to keep up, so he had his crew spread out a sail on
the shore, lay down to wait for conditions to change, and died of
heart failure and/or inhaling volcanic fumes.

If only Pliny the Younger had said more about Rectina. We
must surmise that Rectina was not the woman condemned to
starve because she stole the key to the wine cellar.

8. Galen (129 C.E.-ca. 210 C.E.), *On the Usefulness of Body Parts*:
"Women are more imperfect than men for a very simple
reason: they are colder. If, among the animals, the hottest is the
most active, the coldest must therefore be the most imperfect. In
addition, as noted in dissections, the sexual parts of the woman
are inside the body, while those of the man are outside. It is
important to bear in mind the latter in the discussions on the
equality of men and women."

Pergamon, where Galen was born to a family of means, was a
great hilltop city, capital of a region in Asia Minor (Turkey) whose

last king, having no heir, bequeathed the realm to Rome on his death in 133 B.C.E. to avoid the bloodbath that generally ensued with Roman conquest. Galen grew up enjoying the run of Pergamon's great temples, theaters, stadium, and especially its library, second only to that of Alexandria. Completing his medical studies in Pergamon's world-renowned sanctuary of Asclepius, god of medicine and prophecy, Galen fed his insatiable desire to learn by using wealth inherited from his father, which allowed him to visit medical schools all over the Mediterranean. When the known world had taught Galen everything it could, he returned to Pergamon to become the chief physician at its famed academy for gladiators. There, Galen gained a wealth of information about human anatomy by patching up the gladiators belonging to the High Priest of Asia. Galen's predecessor at the academy had lost sixty gladiators to wounds – Galen only five. The gladiators were of all nations and races. Of course, none were Amazons.

Galen spent some of his career in the service of the co-emperors Marcus Aurelius and Lucius Verus, in the time of Europe's first smallpox epidemic, which came to be named after Galen thanks to his careful description of the disease. In particular, it was identifying the symptoms that allowed predicting whether the patient would live or die that gave Galen fame.

A MIXTURE
OF LIGHT
AND SHADOW

Emerging from the library, leaving behind its depressing ancient "proofs" of woman's inferiority, I looked for ways to use this knowledge, and found myself instead writing about my Island home, the uniqueness of its beauty, unusual things I noticed, in the form of sometimes surrealist poems. At some point during 1959, the poet José Lezama Lima came to my attention. The Island's younger writers and poets, the generation ahead of mine, were attacking Lezama in the cultural weekly *Lunes*, edited by

Guillermo Cabrera Infante and included in the Monday issue of the newspaper *Revolución*. The young poets particularly criticized Lezama for his hermetic style, his obsession with antiquity, and his profound knowledge of Spanish literature of the Golden Age.

I returned to the Lyceum and read all I could by or about Lezama. I was dazzled by his poetry, stunned by his essays. His collection *Analecta del reloj* (*Analects of the Clock*, 1953) was startling, amazing poetry in prose. *Analecta,* along with all my readings at the Lyceum and my life in general, reinforced my desire to write poetry, which had emerged at a very early age. By the year of the Revolution (1959), I'd filled notebooks and began to test my work by submitting a short story to *Lunes*, which was accepted.

To subject my work (that I hadn't burned or cast into the sea) to withering scrutiny, I put together a small book of poems – and had no idea what to do with it. At La Tertulia, the bookstore anybody who cared about writing visited frequently, if only to talk to friends, thumb through books and maybe buy one or two, I sat down to work out where, if anywhere, I fit in. In came the Surrealist poet and literary and art critic Carlos M. Luis, who asked me what I was doing with those piles of books around me. Then he said that Úcar, García & Cía., one of the Island's printers, had just begun accepting entries for its annual poetry competition. The prize was simply that you didn't have to pay them to print your book. Carlos suggested I submit a manuscript of my poems.

I had previously asked Carlos if I might attend the meetings of the *Orígenes* group, which Lezama presided over, surrounded by the best poets of that time and place. Drawn to their poetic universe, I'd read that these conversations were veritable symposia on poetry and literature. Carlos had gently informed me that Lezama did not admit women to the group, except for the poet Fina García Marruz because she was the wife of Lezama's best friend, the poet, essayist and novelist Cintio Vitier, a founding member of the Origenists.

That, of course, set my hair on fire. At age nineteen, in the middle of a communist revolution, in the second half of the 20th century,

PAGE ONE FROM *ANALECTA DEL RELOJ* (1953) BY JOSÉ LEZAMA LIMA: "THE SECRET OF GARCILASO," DEDICATED TO JUAN RAMÓN JIMÉNEZ

Strange Garcilaso.[1] Converted into a pastille, Garcilaso has burned out, but his inhaled fumes have spawned contradictory effects unforeseen by Lopillo.[2] Crystal-clear vapors gathered by the besotted as well as the learned, far from being pretentious or elitist or intended for a specific caste of poets, his influence represents an extraordinary coincidence, one of the strangest of pauses in which distant balances and linkages arrayed themselves. Above and beyond being a dual resolution of the poetic phenomenon, we observe the return of ingenuousness and forced comparisons, how the root of many devotions to the ivory cult conveyed news, apart from any momentary infatuation or seduction, by depicting the materials produced by the popular and the indigenous. We see how the rise of the popular oneiric – troubled by its Thomist conviction in the ultimate reality of all form – even the cultivated architectonic – sensed also by the constant proof of experience, by the fleeting opportunity to grasp the thing – was so coincidental and so desperate, like repairing holes, deficiencies disregarded by the intellect through a seismic sixth sense strangely coincident with earthly drunkenness. With the return of that twofold search came many reciprocal similarities, reverse similarities. "We complain and command," Polo de Medina[3] says in an informal dictum, "that all who desire to eat grapes chew the seeds and don't pick them out with their fingernails, because you'll lose the juicy pulp that clings to the stem." A unifying solution, if by chewing the poetic grapes we might reach the grain's elusive virtue and grace. All the complications and bitter differences arose from hasty gouging by those fingernails, not waiting for the intuited sweetness, or the anxiety that corrodes and warns that the poetic substance should remain hidden or even disappear, rather than continue to exploit the rejuvenated wound in measured doses. We now know that poetry is not something for the exquisite nor for the impressionist's aquarium, but an intimate, sympathetic, bull-sacrificing measure intended to dilute the marmoreal and objective and let them seep through our pores, dissolve our body so that it can become form.

REFERENCES FOR THOSE NOT STEEPED IN SPANISH LITERATURE OF
THE GOLDEN AGE (OR THOSE WHO HAVE NOT [READ] ENOUGH PAGES)

[1] Garcilaso de la Vega: Born in Toledo c. 1501, died in Nice 1536,
Garcilaso introduced the discoveries of Italian Renaissance poetry to
Spanish literature. Soldier and imperial courtier by profession, Garcilaso was an accomplished musician and linguist, and spoke and wrote
Spanish, Latin, Greek, French, and Italian. His poetry embraces classical mythology and Greek and Roman figures, and shuns Catholic
references. His vast influence extends to Spanish-language poets of
today.

[2] Lope Félix de Vega y Carpio: Born in Madrid 1562, died in Madrid
1635, Lope de Vega was a prolific poet, writer of prose, and drama-
tist. Along with his three thousand sonnets, three novels, four novel-
las, nine epic poems, and five hundred plays, his work and that of
Calderón de la Barca and Tirso de Molina transformed the Spanish
language and Spanish theatre. For Lope de Vega's impact on the English theatre, see *The Demetrius Legend and Its Literary Treatment in the Age
of the Baroque* by Ervin C. Brody. At least eighty of Lope's plays continue to be produced worldwide.

[3] Salvador Jacinto Polo de Medina: Born in Murcia, Spain, 1603, died
in 1676, Alcantarilla (Murcia), Polo de Medina was a Baroque poet
and essayist whose best-known work is *Academias del jardín (Academies
of the Garden,* prose and poetry). "Academia Cuarta": "*Iten, sutilizamos
y mandamos que todos los que comieren uvas muerdan del grano y no le arranquen
con los dedos, porque, acontece quedarse alguna parte pegada al palillo.*" Polo de
Medina's wry warning about the scant income poets receive suggests
that those aspiring to that profession avoid the sight of food – for
example, don't live in houses where paintings of fruit adorn the walls,
so as not to be driven mad by hunger. *Obras Completas de Salvador
Jacinto Polo de Medina* (Murcia, Spain: Sucesores de Nogués, 1948), 111.

the last thing I expected to find was social ideas dating back five, or maybe twenty-five, centuries. Of course, paradoxically, like the Origenists, I revered the images and words of antiquity. Unlike the young poets trashing Lezama in *Lunes,* I would have given everything to be a member of Lezama's group, where I thought I could really learn how to be a poet.

When I found out that Lezama had just been named director of the Department of Literature and Publications of the National Council of Culture, I made an appointment to meet him. Since he was the chief juror of the Úcar, García prize, I wanted to see whether he might refuse awarding it to me because I was a woman.

The reception he gave me could not have been colder. The good-humored polymath who had written *Analects of the Clock* was nowhere apparent, at least not to me, and was anything but hermetic about revealing his feelings. I sensed that every word I said made him feel increasingly irritated and trapped. Finally, I gave up trying to talk to him, thanked him for seeing me, and retreated.

Weeks later, Carlos told me that the entire jury had voted for my book over dozens of other entries, and that "probably" I had won the prize. But, he said, now Vitier was quarreling with Lezama, who refused to vote for me because the manuscript was not long enough.

"The book does not have enough pages," Carlos said the great poet kept repeating to any jury member who tried to budge him. Even though Úcar, García's rules for the prize did not specify a number of pages, because Lezama was the Director of the Department of Literature, Lezama's was the only vote that counted. It didn't help when I found out that Lezama's first book, "The Death of Narcissus," which Úcar, García had printed, only had ten pages. Mine had fifty.

Of course poetry isn't measured by weight. Even I knew that.

When I went to retrieve the manuscript at Úcar, García's, the janitor looked up from mopping the hall floor. "They were arguing for days about a young lady's book, but the Fat Man kept saying he wouldn't give it his vote because it didn't have enough pages," he said.

Which was exactly what Carlos had told me.

§

From the window of the Pan American flight I took to leave the Island, I could see a column of militia men marching on the brown surface of the earth, streaked with tropical green. Militia men marching mechanically and in unison like Belial's army, turned into Sisyphus by now heading right, then again left, never advancing. The soldiers' rifles gleamed under the Caribbean sun like fangs bared, ready to devour, ready to morph into a barbed-wire fence around the entire coastline of the Island, converting it into a prison encircled by the sea.

§

The past had turned into a black well whose brick wall I could peer over and look down to see, immortalized in black, gray, bright-white celluloid, a woman crying in the rain.

Veronica Voss, the actress, has been commenting on how cinema works – mingling paranoid obsession with philosophical depth and poetic imagination. A morphine addict, she lies, begs, conceals, play-acts to get drugs, and she's not alone. To the clinic, which is both "home" where she lives and her prison of stupor, go all those who want to forget their nightmares. Her neurologist's talent is insatiable greed: she provides patients with morphine in exchange for money, property – everything they own, including their lives. An elderly Jewish couple who survived the camps surrender their lives and possessions to forget images of the past that haunt them; Veronica Voss sells her own life in exchange for obliterating a present she can't endure.

As the actress, within hours of her death, stands at the piano, seemingly seductive and famous among the infernal characters encircling her, she sings "Memories are Made of This." Her Teutonic blonde wig, backlit for a spectral glow, is cropped by the screen; her lips almost sketch a smile, and she seems to meditate on words she's uttered only moments before: "Why's the whole world so afraid of death? Life – it's life that's so strange . . ."

Haloed by the room's lights in that luxurious house/clinic, by jewel-adorned women draped in finery, by the coarse and greedy men of film-making, overcome in that glorious moment when she's surrounded by luxury, by promise – by the illusion – of success, she thinks of other words she's uttered that night about the cinema and which, now, will send her off on her trip to eternity: "It's all a mixture of light and shadow; nothing more."

How different is the lamentation of the objectified diva past her prime from the resentment of the young poet at being a victim of gender prejudice carried down through the ages, or of subsequently encountered prejudices about birthplace, sexual orientation, political thinking. And yet there they all are, somehow linked, until we reach that realization: "It's all a mixture of light and shadow."

Whether there is anything more remains to be seen.

MUSICAL MOMENTS

I

The house lights dim. A reddish glow from some tiny bulbs reflects in the gold leaf on the walls and the cloth-of-gold curtains. Time takes up space, becomes corporeal, tangible, and I think of the ten thousand things I would be doing at this moment if I were not listening, in this baroque theater, to the perfect development of the mimetic counterpoint in Bach's fugues. Those ten thousand things turn into anxiety and agitate my perceptive capacity to such a pitch that I imagine I've been invaded by a virulent fever, of the sort that wiped out entire towns during the Middle Ages. This makes the music seem to be coming from every direction and the performers just pretending to play: the music creates itself and emerges spontaneously from the core of the ether, reaching my ears amplified by supernatural loudspeakers that don't increase decibels but rather degrees of meaning. This means that I have to experience the music physically: my memory feels the first chord from the piano followed by the ascending and descending arpeggios from the violin of César Franck's *Sonata for Violin and Piano*, about which Vincent d'Indy said, in his *Traité de composition*, it was "the first and purest model of the cyclical treatment of themes in the form of an instrumental sonata." That arpeggio has been identified, as well, with the little phrase of the violin – the so-called "birdsong" – in the sonata of Vinteuil that so obsessed Swann in Marcel Proust's novel *In Search of Lost Time*. Others, however, connect that little phrase with the main theme of the first movement of Saint-Saëns' *Sonata for Violin in C Minor*.

The music of my memory begins to create shapes, to color images. A blue stripe sketches the sky of an afternoon on the Island; another, slightly green, recreates the constant presence of the sea by outlining the horizon. My hand hurls papers into the sea, small notes like classified ads: "Seeking Seamstress Skilled in Singer Sewing Machines." Sometimes, for a change, I toss poems written in Greek, copied out of a book in the National Library.

These Greek poems I throw into the sea are written on bits of paper while behind me they are beating the bongo. It is a spectacular afternoon; the sky fans out a range of colors from red to violet, and the transparent sea, with greenish filaments that cling to the stones in its depths and ebb and flow with the waves, emanates a pungent and salty odor. I am the only person sitting on the Malecón gazing out at the sea; everyone around me is focused on the city. They gossip about their neighbors, describe the fabric they bought from the Poles on Muralla Street. From the three-story buildings behind me, the sound of a conga drum emerges to accompany the bongos: the rhythm of this happy city that's soon to be covered by a layer of depression and blackness, but now, in my memory, it is resplendent.

I perceive myself as a neurotic obsessively watching how our iridescent portion of the Atlantic Ocean breaks against the reefs of the Malecón. Some men passing by in a convertible shout "Jump!" They assume I'm suicidal: it's a tropical syllogism that the only people in this country who look at the sea are those planning to commit suicide, just as they only look at fires when they plan to set themselves alight. However, not even suicide makes them original because they always leave the same note, to be published in the Island newspapers' obits: "I killed myself because I am bored with life. Let no one be blamed for my death." Antithetically to the insular custom, I have no desire to commit suicide. I am launching sheets of paper because I'm possessed by the Dionysian frenzy that causes me to receive, through the very pores of my skin, an exuberant landscape, a rainbow of images, fragrances, textures.

II

The birdsong in Franck's sonata opens the door of my imagination. I keep hearing that arpeggio at transcendent moments, in which I interrupt the drama of the instant to pay attention to the violin's notes and, even more closely, to the performance of the violinist playing in my memory, as well as the deep, meditative notes of the accompanying piano. At those times I'm staring, frozen, like Liv Ullman in *Persona* when, playing Electra on stage, she freezes and stops talking forever. I'm overcome with awe listening to sounds that travel through the tunnel of time, embellished, made superhuman, apotheosized – notes of the imagination.

Everything ceases to matter; only music is essential, its sound carrying a multitude of images: night in the desert, cold brought on by a dry wind that blows dust from the dunes, the moon lighting up those immobile waves of sand.

Before obsessing about Franck's sonata, the music that I listened to in my imagination was a motley mix that did not spring up at those transcendent moments, but rather assaulted me suddenly, at the most prosaic moments. When I made an effort to learn how to operate an IBM key punch machine at the Commerce Arcade (one of my famous practical projects), I almost went crazy when, as soon as they turned on the machines, I heard Chopin's *Andante Spianato and Grande Polonaise Brillante* played by a hundred pianos arranged acoustically the way the pianist Liberace was greeted in the 1950s at the airport then named Rancho Boyeros. Needless to say, I didn't pass the Commerce Arcade's graduation exam taken by the Island's thousands of excellent IBM key punch operators. The thunderous noise produced by those people gone berserk with their odious speed in taking the exam threw me into a paroxysm of despair. I felt trapped in one of my stupid dreams in which I am selling fish in a people's market in Sweden and, humiliatingly, am unable to hawk the goods in Swedish. Or those other dreams where I go into a bathroom in the business district of Oslo, Norway, where savage crowds of seated women keep crossing and uncrossing their legs, smoking, inspecting their mascara in the mirrors, leafing through fashion magazines with primal impatience, interrogating anybody who comes in about what they did or didn't do that week in bed. Or nightmares like the one about the beauty salon in La Víbora, where ladies go to have streaks put in their hair – streaks like neon lights, in all the colors of the solar spectrum, sprouting from the capillaries of their scalps, making these women who seek perfection in a hair salon look like the succubae of Hieronymus Bosch decked out in hallucinatory Botticellian curls.

Another of my "practical" projects sabotaged by music was to learn shorthand at the Nobel Academy. Just then the University of Havana had been closed, following an attack on the Presidential Palace led by a faction of the Student Directorate. Thus, suddenly, the Nobel Academy filled up with clueless people taking a little practical break from their academic/professional studies, in which they set out to learn "business skills." Unfortunately for me, in that chaos, my study of shorthand became confused with a trio for piano, violin, and cello by Édouard Lalo, rarely played and infrequently recorded. This trio took possession of me every time I ought to have been memorizing the lines and curves essential for producing the symbols so ingeniously invented by Gregg. My musical reveries resulted in symbols so complicated that the instructor suggested that, to develop speed, might I just write the words longhand?

III

The sweet, satanic sadness of Liszt's *Mephisto Waltz*, suggestive of scenes of demons condemned to eternal copulation, deriving from it no other pleasure than that of wallowing in concupiscence as an affront to the Divinity, is what I hear in my memory during the vigils at the Monument to the Medical Students. (These were eight innocent young men matriculated in the medical school who were executed in 1871 after being falsely accused of profaning the tomb of a Spanish journalist, an incident that led to the Island becoming, briefly, a possession of the United States.) A rumor circulating among a group of Island intellectuals and visionaries insinuates that the angel belonging to this funerary monument has been observed batting its eyelashes. The image of this blinking marble angel takes possession of my nights, which I spend lying on the pavement in front of the angel with eyes wide open and unblinking, determined to catch any movement, no matter how slight or near-imperceptible, of those stone eyelids.

Sometimes young soldiers approach to ask me the time. I carefully observe their boots, shiny as mirrors, their clear faces with rosy, bulging, seraphic cheeks that reflect that peculiar, unconditional dedication of youth to the present moment. Nubile faces that play at Life and Death by rolling the dice. No one ever asks me what I'm doing prone on the pavement, staring at a statue in the asphyxiating, desolate nights of the Island.

IV

On the Day of the Dead all music leaves me, and I can only hear the pregnant silence that sound leaves in its wake. I get off the bus at the Cemetery of Columbus, in which, incongruously,

Columbus is not buried. I let the crowd drag me along in its surge towards the marble tombs.

I manage, though barely, the purchase of a bouquet of flowers before abruptly being carried off in a foaming whirlpool of mourners moving around the lavish mortuary constructions that the Islanders have erected. I read somewhere that, next to the one in Florence, this cemetery is the most baroque in the world. I believe it, because its Berninian creations have always astonished me: pyramids of granite with divine Masonic eyes framed by the spread compass of the Great Architect; opulent mausoleums that squander Carrara marble on the sidewalks surrounding the structures; artistic grilles brocaded with Byzantine and Moorish designs, abundances of arabesques and Mozarabic volutes interwoven with foliage.

My favorite tombs are those displaying sepia photographs of wasp-waisted women of exaggerated bust under antique silk and muslin gowns; boys dressed as sailors, their locks combed into curls, rolling a hoop along the ground with a stick; Herculean young men with handlebar mustaches and clear, transparent eyes that seem enlightened by contemplating the infinity of the tomb in which, after so much noise and bluster, they've been laid to rest.

The cemetery is the only private place on the Island, that cradle of extroverts, and the only place I can, as they say in English, "hear myself think." Here, finally, everybody's calmed down, and not even the throngs of visitors dare violate that solemn silence in which the dead take such delight. In the cemetery I stop imagining sounds and only hear the harmonic, musical silence, the profundity of the quiet, its inaudible high-frequency vibration, like the pause between two notes.

I go, almost blindly, to the tomb of Luisa Pérez de Zambrano to deposit the flowers I bought in our dizzying pass by the florist, propelled by a drunken crowd obsessed with their dead forebears.

Luisa's tomb is in a state of sad neglect: cracked marble, with roots and bushes slithering through the cracks, dead flowers in plastic vases. An impressive gilded funerary plaque dominates the scene, gift of Mallén Zambrano in honor of her relative, whom José Martí regarded as the Island's greatest elegiac poet.

I am indignant at the deterioration of the tomb of this pitiable great poet who reputedly died of hunger. (Recent commentators have wondered how this could be so, given the size of the mansion she lived in after the death of her husband and five sons.) By contrast, the dazzling golden plaque shines with appalling irony on this tomb that preserves the mortal remains of an extraordinary woman devastated by bad luck.

The shadows of visitors who've stayed late with their dead cut silhouettes on the horizon. They look like penitent ghosts in a funeral march, maintaining a biting, leaden silence impossible to break into.

A woman dressed in black approaches the tomb and asks, "Are you a relative of Luisa's?"

"No," I say.

"Of Mallén's, then?"

"No. I write poems."

I feel compelled to give her that absurd explanation. What is the connection between writing poems and tidying up a grave? No matter – the explanation pacifies the woman. After all, cleaning graves of people you don't know is almost as weird as writing poems.

"Don't forget to visit Mallén – she lives on Calzada. Tell her you're the one from the tomb."

The woman rejoins her group of silent walkers whom the shadows will quickly devour.

V

On occasion, to avoid listening to a specific musical piece that haunts me in connection with someone I can't eliminate from my life, I have even stopped going to concerts and turned off the radio – and yet the theme will spring from someone whistling, a waitress singing as she serves a pizza, or the radio of a car stopped beside me while I wait for the light to change. The worst is to hear the song in my head. There is no way to stop it; it's auditory dementia, of the sort that Schumann suffered from the note *mi*. Some say he had tinnitus.

While I lived in Puerto Rico, I would hear in my mind the *Agnus Dei*, the last of the major sections of the ordinary mass, when I was going to meet my friend Vicente, a well-known Puerto Rican lawyer. If I heard the *Agnus Dei* in the morning, I never bought lunch because I knew I would run into Vicente, who always invited me to eat.

One day, sitting in my office in Old San Juan correcting an article I had deliriously translated from Italian, I heard Fauré's *Agnus Dei*. I enjoyed this exquisitely absurd moment of having written something nobody was going to read, for a weekly magazine that was thrown away as soon as it was distributed. Four children from the poverty-stricken district of La Perla delivered the weekly in record time, and people took even less time to throw it away. Sometimes, excited, I ran out of the office when my boss told me they were distributing the weekly, but I was never fast enough to get a copy. Probably it was just as well, since my translation of articles from Italian and French magazines into Spanish was creative: I invented the stories. Why repeat what's already been published? Thus came into being the inspiring stories of the young man from Reggio Calabria who saw the Virgin standing in his shoes and decided he must walk barefoot; the clandestine relationship between Juliette Greco and the Nazis; the secret diary of Sartre's illegitimate son.

Inspired mainly by articles in *Corriere della Sera* and *Paris Match*, I crafted stories of prodigious happenings, re-cast for the tropical imagination. One morning I was writing an article, intensely pleased with myself. As I did every morning, I rested my eyes on the Atlantic Ocean at its most spectacular. I'd arrived on the bus to Old San Juan in time for breakfast at Cafetería Mallorca, *criollo* coffee accompanied by the shop's famed *mallorcas*, sweet buns topped with butter and dusted with powdered sugar. The magical city of Old San Juan smelled of spices, tropics, books – future.

Typing away, I was living an existential moment; as Albert Camus said of the Spaniards, I was "caught right in the act of existing," when I heard the chorus singing the *Agnus Dei* from Fauré's *Requiem* in my imagination, and I knew I was going to see Vicente. I ran out of the office, and around the corner bumped into him. Vicente invited me to a chicken *asopao* at a restaurant that specializes in preparing that typical Puerto Rican dish, which is served in metal jars.

Between anecdotes, jokes, and stories, Vicente urges me to meditate in the mountains with an esoteric group of Sun worshipers, devotees of an American reverend who left her lucrative photography studio on Fifth Avenue in New York for the mysticism of the mountains of Puerto Rico's central mountain range. The reverend's successful career was destroyed when she began photographing spirits that appeared behind the socialites and magnates as she was taking their portraits. Her elegant clientele left her, horrified at this inappropriate intrusion from the Beyond.

VI

Within moments dawn will arrive. The Sun Worshipers are awake and have quietly covered themselves with white robes. Since I have not brought any such garments, I decide to throw on a sheet, arranged as mystically as possible.

The last thing I ever imagined was that I might climb a mountain, shortly before dawn, wrapped in a sheet, and be destined to honor the Sun. I had read of the obsession of Amenhotep IV with Amun Ra, the Egyptian solar god, and seen in books the bas reliefs from Amarna, where the rays of the Sun – the Aten – ended in magnetic little hands that projected creative energy, but I never thought that I would participate in a religious rite of Akhenaten in modern Puerto Rico.

The worshipers light the way with white candles.

The night is still dark, and I half-see the faces of the people in the reddish light of the flames. A vast silence reigns as we follow the Reverend up the stony slope. No sound comes from the birds or crickets, no howls of wild animals: all of creation is silent, in suspense, apprehensive that the Sun might not appear this morning. Reaching the peak, we all stand in a circle and look towards the East. The sky turns cerulean and, from behind the threatening blackness of nearby mountain tops, the first ray of light flies out, crosses the plain, illuminating in passing the uppermost jungle canopy and the throats of birds, which, in unison, burst forth in jubilant song.

DEFORMED BY PHILOSOPHY

I

The young man stood up, pushed back his desk, and stormed out of the classroom, shouting: "What in hell do Wittgenstein and the Logical Positivists know about the anguish of a lonely heart!"

Nobody in the class said a word. I recorded that instant in my mind because I thought something had become clear. Here was this undergraduate, this beautiful young man with curly black hair who evidently enjoyed being in the prime of his life, savoring his youth and his classical Greek beauty – how could I feel sorry for him? That romantic explosion seemed to me an inexcusable lack of discipline, of rigor, an atrocious display by a spoiled brat. On the other hand, it was pretty spectacular, even extraordinary. The young man who'd walked out of the class with that rebellious gesture had told the professor, Dr. Rudolf von Frege, eminence of philosophy and luminary among the great philosophical brains of the Vienna Circle, to shut up because everything he was saying deeply offended the lonely heart.

Frege raised his hands towards the ceiling as if giving up hope in the face of the intellectual limitations of our tropical neurons. I felt compassion for him. Here he was, having to teach philosophy at the University of Puerto Rico because of his health. Clearly, he hadn't given thought to what repairing his body might do to his mind.

Frege had invited me to attend his class because he had read my second novel and told a mutual friend, Marta Urquiza, a professor of French Language and Literature at the university, cousin of the Chilean poet Vicente Urquiza, that he would love to have me in his class. Why did this Austrian genius want me in his class? The truth is, I still have no idea. I never found out because we never spoke. To talk to him would have been to destroy the mystery of his class: that distressing struggle of Theseus against the Minotaur. On the other hand, it was not pleasant to watch a genius losing his marbles and not be able to do a thing about it. But what could I do? I was no luminary of philosophy. Did he want me to ask smart questions? I couldn't think of any questions, intelligent or stupid. All I could do in class was laugh.

After the departure of the young man, several minutes passed in which perplexity reigned. Frege looked lost, like a puppet whose strings had been cut. I wanted to help him. I wanted to tell him that the tropical Adonis's solitary heart was of no importance. That heart was going to be devoured by worms, whereas Frege's lucid and penetrating intelligence would shine for ever and ever. Wherever in the world humanity cared about philosophy, his studies would be mentioned. I also thought about what had caused the Adonis to explode: the philosophy of poor Wittgenstein, who day after day tried to keep himself alive by explaining the world to itself. Here was a man so obsessed with the idea of suicide – who, like Søren Kierkegaard, had this sting in the flesh, this hidden torment that nobody has been able to discover – who was so antisocial that no one, not even charitable souls, could bear talking to him for more than fifteen minutes – and who, to make himself feel better, set about explaining everything.

Wittgenstein, like Frege, had no love for teaching. He forbade his students to take notes, and refused to teach in the claustrophobic space of a classroom. He lectured in his rooms at Cambridge. His classes were like séances with the genie of philosophy. When he fell into a trance, no one was allowed to interrupt him. And no one could have, because no one understood a word of what he was saying.

In like manner, no one understood a word of what Frege taught.

Except me. I understood him, modesty aside, and to my eternal embarrassment, because I could not help him with his students who tormented him. I was prevented by my sense of humor and the whimsical way my brain works. And if I did understand him, it was not because I had special ability, but because his class was fun for me, while for the rest of the students it was torture. Years later, while suffering in some of the demeaning jobs I'd had to take, I understood that mysterious stupidity produced by supreme disgust at being forced to do something one detests. Stupidity acts as a defense mechanism, a capsule of armor against which alien concepts crash and disintegrate. Wrapped in their capsules, most of Frege's students were unenthusiastic about contemplating a philosophy that made no sense whatever, and yet everyone in the class was supposedly majoring in Philosophy. But I could understand with an open mind since I did not aspire to become a philosopher. And it made perfect sense to me to just sit back and enjoy the exquisite distillations of Frege's mind, absorb his philosophical testament to the world.

During the pause created by the young man's obnoxious exit, I looked out the window: the trees of the university's beautiful campus looked so peaceful in the late afternoon light, their leaves moving gently in the evening breeze that mixed the subtle smell of spices coming from the student cafeteria with the penetrating and oily perfume of nocturnal flowers just beginning to open their petals.

What were we doing in that class? — shut away inside four walls, while out of doors life spread out exuberantly and intoxicated those who surrendered to it? I knew that the idealization of Nature I was feeling at that moment had arisen in the Renaissance and became fashionable during German Romanticism, particularly when Goethe used it to describe the sufferings of young Werther. But for me, the brief flicker of that moment revealed a new reality, authentic and palpable. I wanted — just then — to absorb existence, fill myself with life, enjoy its meaning, experience its splendor. I lived in a constant hyperbole of perceptions and desires. I felt, and could almost grasp with my hands, a fullness of perception and joy whose climax always escaped me, but left a trail behind itself that renewed my thirst and spurred on my despair.

Frege pulled me out of my reverie by making a lot of noise erasing the blackboard, which, curiously, had already been erased. Frege seemed to be trying to spread the whitish trace of the chalk evenly across the surface of the slate and, at the same time, submerge himself in his intellect so he could continue his discourse on the concept of the play of language in Wittgenstein's thought.

II

Mercedes Wise was waiting for me in the cafeteria after class. She had placed the little woven purse she always carried on my chair to save my seat, and now lit a cigarette with a brusque gesture.

"You always have to laugh in class," she said, incensed. "You have no conception of the seriousness of these philosophical ideas. And don't go dragging up some anecdote to support your interpretation of what just happened, some ridiculous literary explanation."

I sat down, resigned to having another of those ritual conversations with which we kept ourselves entertained.

"You keep forgetting I don't want to be a philosophy professor," I replied. "I'm in this class by accident, like the mule who found he could play the flute. If I don't talk about philosophy, it's not because I perversely avoid the subject, but because my mind runs in crazy anti-philosophical lines."

"Your second novel is *a philosophical study*," said Wise tartly.

"My second novel is full of contradictions. It has no structure or logical development of ideas."

"You're afflicted with the affectation of peasants. In other words, you play the fool. You know perfectly well that only philosophy can be said to have contradictions. Don't you find Nietzsche full of contradictions? *Thus Spoke Zarathustra* is crammed with contradictions. Wittgenstein himself, after the *Tractatus logico-philosophicus*, expressed his philosophy in the form of small aphorisms without structure or logical development of ideas, better suited to his mentality than philosophically developing an argument. Remember that, as regards contradictions, *Philosophical Investigations* completely contradicts the thesis of the *Tractatus*."

I looked at her curiously. I seemed to have tuned into a TV soap opera with Mexican actresses spouting hallucinatory monologues. This conversation we were having was completely surreal in the context of the University of Puerto Rico. We were surrounded by young men full of energy who wore white cotton shirts and starched khakis that made a muffled crackling sound when they got up or sat down at the tables (something they were constantly inspired to do by their animal energy in rebellion against the torpor of autocratic old professors, the boredom of studying, and the nitpicking of intellectualism). Tanned young men, with bodies that rose in reverse pyramids encased in white shirts and finished in heads that were a continuation of their massive necks adorned with bulging veins, dominated the scene. Their blond or black locks fell on broad, clear foreheads atop faces that ended in square jaws thrust toward the future, like the heroic youths of Soviet Realist posters of the 1930s. The women, in the background like a Greek chorus, spoke with complicity and jangled their bracelets, laughing and fluttering their false eyelashes. I was obsessed with those plastic bracelets that came in all colors and patterns. I was intrigued, too, by the fate of their owners who dreamed now, while they ate their evening meals of rice and beans, of inaccessible earthly landscapes and unbridled passions they only dared to imagine while reading the latest crop of romance novels.

"Don't you think, Wise, we've become a little byzantine? Look at the landscape: coconut palms and banana trees, a young man strumming a guitar. Enjoy the sweet smell of fried ripe plantains that fills this cafeteria. Does any of this have the slightest thing to do with what we're talking about?"

Wise flicked the ash from her cigarette into the white saucer she had placed strategically next to her books. Her fingers were long and thin, ending in long, well-groomed nails. Her veins looked blue and violet, bulging under her tanned skin. Wise was an enigma. I never knew what she was going to say, and it seemed to me that her thoughts and emotions took shape in a pool of boiling lava, emerging in viscous bubbles that, when Wise spoke, exploded and burned everything they touched. These telluric mysteries frustrated me, and for that reason we spent a lot of time not talking, plunged into absolute desolation.

"Why don't we change the subject," she said.

III

In those days the most insignificant scenes, like the one in the cafeteria, gave off a mysterious psychic vibration. It seemed that something secret was always going on behind the facts that I could not understand, but if I had been able to decipher them, worlds would be explained. I was determined to penetrate that other side, so pregnant with the significance of instants.

Along with that wish, I had a strange confidence in what the future might bring. Although I was always accompanied by a sacred psychic reverberation, I felt that everything I experienced at the time was simply a prologue to Life, which would soon begin. When Life materialized, everything was going to be different. I would then be able to fully experience existence and understand its meaning. I had no idea what I was doing and I did not want to cling to easy solutions having to do with work, studies, and family. I was always stunned and astonished at the abyss, but I knew that situation was temporary. There was a Divinity that would speak through the Oracle, and a Destiny that would come from the future, which, one day, had to open its doors. All I had to do at that moment was to wake up from the dream of everyday life and pass through the doors of Revelation.

It was Marta Urquiza who touched this chord of dazzling predestination with great virtuosity every time we spoke.

On certain triumphant days, bursting with ideas about the bright future, I would set off to visit Marta, to validate my exaggerated dreams. Marta lived in the apartment building that housed a large part of the faculty of the University of Puerto Rico, behind the buildings where classes were held. A professor of French, Marta also loved literature written in Spanish.

Whenever I arrived, Marta would be waiting for me with an air of longing, as if she were about to make her entrance on stage.

"I just read your novel for the second time, Mercedes. I know that you fly with your own wings and that you fly high."

Her words were not meant to be complimentary. She attacked subjects with scientific precision, coincidentally providing a healing, soothing balm for wounds that the spirit might suffer because of incomprehension, envy, cruelty. Marta had that gift of hitting the nail on the head and at the same time preserving admirable intellectual integrity. I never thought she was flattering me, or that she wanted something from me. Her words of praise flowed from her essence, like blood pressed out of a duck to make *canard à l'orange*. Marta had drained out all the blood and spoke with a certain pain, as if words were parts of her own body that she had to give me, driven by the iron hand of literary justice. Her pain was not based on envy or jealousy, but on critical rigor.

"Why don't we talk about Vicente Urquiza instead," I said, embarrassed, to move us over to Marta's favorite topic.

"Ah! – Now, *Vicente* was a seducer," Marta began, savoring the words as if they were a succulent dish. "And his seduction, like the cape of a magician from *The Thousand and One Nights*, spread out over everyone who was around him. It didn't matter to him that I was a simple fourteen-year-old girl – he *had* to seduce me. He told me the most fascinating stories about his time in Paris: anecdotes about Picabia, the clever tricks of André Breton. Vicente had a sumptuous apartment in Paris, on the Right Bank. That was his golden age. Everything changed afterwards, when he returned to Chile, and, at the end of his life, fell out of favor with

Chilean society because he kidnapped and later married a young woman who could have been his daughter. That was when I got in touch with him. He could talk for hours about his life in Paris, reliving it to protect himself against the sadness of his later years."

She paused, then added, "Something like this is happening to Frege."

The coquí frogs began their nightly chorus. Outside, night was falling and shadows filtered through the blinds. I visualized the tropical twilight's swagger dissolving into tender, morose night, soft around the edges, suffusing everything with a joyous mystery.

"Frege is obsessed with the Vienna Circle," Marta went on. "He talks all the time about Wittgenstein – manically. He's made the man into a fetish. He's united his life with that Viennese philosopher's in some magical way, as if he's the ventriloquist and Wittgenstein is the dummy. Now, Frege listens only to Schubert, Wittgenstein's favorite composer. He dreams he has a fortune that he will donate to his siblings." (Inspired by reading Tolstoy's *Gospels*, Wittgenstein had come to consider his vast wealth a burden. He divided it among his siblings, because they were already rich and he did not want to corrupt a poor person with a sudden influx of great wealth.)

Marta was thirty years older than Wise; however, they resembled each other in their capacity for synthesis, in their ability to concentrate like a laser on an idea or observation. This similarity I don't think was due to the fact that they were friends and had learned from each other, but rather to a spiritual affinity that had nothing to do with material things. Marta's powers of concentration were such that she became completely absorbed and never noticed what was around her, an intensity that enveloped her listeners to such a degree that, for example, I have no recollection of her house, or the clothes she wore, or what she looked like physically: only the impression of her, and her insightful comments, remain in my memory.

When talking about Frege, Marta always lowered her voice as if describing something sinful, unveiling some tragic premonition.

"Frege lives above life and doesn't prop himself up, unlike us, with sublime or grotesque fantasies, but with his all-absorbing meditation on Wittgenstein. He's managed to construct some magical coordinates that join his life to that of the philosopher, coordinates that 'go through him like a ray – a thread – of light, and then, suddenly, it gets dark,' as Salvatore Quasimodo would say. He doesn't want to acknowledge what that philosophy class costs him – or maybe he does see it, but he can't find another solution to his economic problem."

"Maybe the philosophy class is his salvation," I said. "It gives him something to do."

IV

We were in a hotel restaurant in the elegant neighborhood of El Condado. A few round tables, metal, painted white and topped with glass, under white umbrellas with red stripes, made up the *al fresco* restaurant overlooking the Atlantic Ocean, whose waters broke majestically against the reefs. It was one of those slow and comforting afternoons that I had the good fortune to be able to enjoy then. Wise and I had banana daiquiris. The sky was spectacular, with those dramatic green and mauve tones so characteristic of the Antilles. The breeze coming from the ocean was warm, full of penetrating but pleasant marine smells. An air of expectation set the environment alight, as if something important was on the verge of being created or discovered.

"Frege is giving me private lessons. It's tutoring, like they have at Cambridge, he says."

Wise delivered that information like dropping a depth bomb. She wanted to know what effect it would cause.

"Of course he's not doing it to emulate Wittgenstein," I joked.

Now, she seemed embarrassed. "Not at all," she said. "He says he wants to explain to me in more detail what he says in class."

Well, why? Of course I thought this "tutoring" had nothing whatever to do with philosophical interest.

The afternoon lulled the senses and made me settle into life like a feather cushion, to which Wise's conversation was like the annoying pea under the mattress. But I could not avoid hearing what she said. I had to follow the conversational cycle which, once begun, would not end until its natural conclusion. Life was escaping through the fissures in that instant, and Death was hurling warning darts at me about the brevity of existence: I was wasting time.

"Frege is obsessed with the Vienna Circle," whispered Wise. "I think he gives me those classes so I can hear his thoughts. He talks so fast, it's like he has a tornado in his head, sucking out his brain."

"Can't you imagine his problem is us? He's like Gulliver in the Land of the Lilliputians! Think: none of us has his background, or his intellectual capacity, and he's supposed to share his ideas with those of us around him. What could be more exasperating?"

The afternoon breeze started to cool. The change of temperature brought a touch of lightness to the tone of our conversation.

"I think he clings to my youth. Frege is a young man in an old body. I mean, his enthusiasm, the novelty of his ideas! No young person can compare to him. They're all empty – those smooth faces, those shallow glances."

"You're kind of hard on our young men!"

Wise took a sip of her daiquiri, tossing her thick brown hair back and forth as if to free her brain of cobwebs. I admired her judgment. It was great to be able to judge people like that, with self-assurance and security. This ability could only come into being in a beautiful young woman, pampered by men who, amused by her charm, excused all her excesses. And yet, despite all these advantages, Wise was not at all vain and had an uncommon amount of self-discipline.

"Frege is behaving symbolically. It's Wagnerian: his life is an art that unites all the arts. He's recapturing his youth through me," Wise said in a low voice.

V

In the dead silence of all of us holding our breath while Frege, eyes closed, face raised to heaven, hands piously joined on his chest like an El Greco saint, gathered his wits to start the class, the lonely-hearted young man burst in with the noise of the door slamming and a chair scraping on the floor.

He had missed several weeks of classes and suddenly there he was, late and causing a ruckus. Without looking at anyone, he sat down beside Wise and took out his notebook. Frege, immersed in his introspection, ignored the noise, made louder by the tension it caused, as if this was beneath dignifying it with his thoughts.

"Samuel Beckett is the best exponent of Wittgenstein's philosophy," he said quietly, as if talking in a dream, "because he does not speak to us about the emptiness of existence but makes us live it."

During the entire hour the class lasted, Frege spoke brilliantly about the Theater of the Absurd and its relation to Logical Positivism. Wise took notes furiously, while the lonely-hearted young man studied her profile.

After class we went to the student cafeteria. We sat quietly, Wise, the Adonis and I, around a table in a secluded corner, far from the groups of students who liked to talk about sports and politics in loud voices.

"Wittgenstein is a colossal sophist," the Adonis all of a sudden adjudicated. "His philosophy is a crock because it contains its own contradiction."

"Yes," I said, "why you can't talk about what isn't verifiable, when this is the only thing worth talking about."

"Wittgenstein does not preclude talking about what's not verifiable," Wise snapped at me viciously. "He just warns us that the unverifiable doesn't merit consideration because it's mere metaphysics."

The Adonis got up suddenly with great energy and, to make his point more obvious, without saying a word went to the cigarette machine. He returned with a pack of Salems, holding it with both hands and with all his muscles tensed, as if weighed a ton. The way he moved was uninhibited and proclaimed that the whole space belonged to him. By returning to our table, he had dominated the cafeteria and taken by assault the table, the chairs, and Wise.

I looked at Wise curiously to gauge her susceptibility to this type of feral domination tactics. Wise looked down. The index and middle fingers of her right hand that held her lit cigarette were trembling.

VI

We were listening to a Mozart sonata in Wise's bedroom. We were alone. We had closed the door so that we would not be disturbed by the sounds that came from the dining room, announcing the preparation of dinner. We had not turned on the light and the room was only illuminated by the street lamps, whose light entered timidly through the slats of the Venetian blinds and projected mostly on the ceiling. A strange reddish glow came from the lights on the turntable's control panel. Wise seemed to suffer in the gloom.

"You just *had* to agree with him about Wittgenstein," Wise said.

"Really? Is it fair to send someone into battle who's already been sentenced to death? You know perfectly that if I'd won the argument, you'd have felt sorry for him, and if I'd lost, you would have despised me."

"Monster! You are such a monster! – when will I understand you!" Wise exclaimed.

Mozart's sonata seemed to have been composed for that moment. The music was engaging in a secret conversation with us. The pianist played slowly, each note caressed until squeezed of all its sap, its pitch of torn nostalgia, of longing so vast that human understanding couldn't encompass it.

VII

Marta Urquiza sat down, keeping her back very erect and crossing her legs in a theatrical gesture that I thought fit for a Sarah Bernhardt. There was something flamboyant, at the same time subtle, in the way she sat, her ceremonious way of starting a particularly interesting conversation.

"Mercedes, Vicente's father, who's almost 100 years old, read your book of poems before starting dinner. I just received his letter from Chile where he tells me, with great style and tasty details, what I'm telling you in my brief and pedestrian way. My family was so very moved that you dedicated your book to our poet who persists, not only in photos but in our family memory, as the most eminent among us."

"I owe him a great deal. I've always paid, in one way or the other, all the writers who were important to me in my adolescence."

Marta nodded impatiently, as if telling me she knew very well what I was saying and, at the same time, was passionately in agreement. Her gesture proclaimed a complicity and, at the same time, a compliment. That afternoon there was something odd in the air, as if we were already done with all the overtures and were about to launch into naked communication. Marta had always kept her distance and appreciated that I kept mine, which allowed us to explore all kinds of topics without getting intellectually bored, or emotionally overwhelmed. We had achieved a refreshing Cartesian space in the midst of the asphyxiating tropics of human relationships. But now I feared that plunge into naked communication: I had seen it fail so many times!

"Mercedes, you who are capable of dedicating a book to a dead man, important as he was to our esoteric Andean literature, and then to send it to his family to tug at their heartstrings just before dinner, to remind them of him whose last name I bear, and who left the fruit of his efforts in works written in two great Romance languages – maybe you can understand the subtle vibration that's taken possession of me this afternoon."

"I don't understand that vibration. There are times when being obtuse turns out to be prudent," I said, trying to lighten the heavy atmosphere of impending confession.

"I feel the vibration that comes from our philosophical zone," she continued without listening to me. "I intuit what is happening: ships foundering, great winds, a terrible sensation of the vanity of all things."

When she finished saying this, which I somehow picked up was not what she wanted to confide in me, Marta changed the subject suddenly, as if trying to erase the words she had said in an apparent faux-pas. Soon after, I left because, really, our communication was over. When I left, I turned around and saw Marta looking at me through the window as if she were a prisoner with no possibility of escape, and as if I had been her last hope and was irretrievably slipping out of her hands.

VIII

On entering the class, Wise whispered in my ear: "Marta's husband left her. She's packing her bags and going back to Chile." Telling me this, she sat down next to me, capriciously, since her desk was behind mine. I prayed silently to the divinities of discretion that she wouldn't continue to whisper in my ear the life and miracles of Marta Urquiza.

The Adonis made another of his triumphal entries and sat down next to Wise, exerting his usual tactics of territorial domination. Wise, briefly flustered, took out her notebook and anxiously waited for Frege to make his appearance.

A few minutes passed and Frege arrived. The whole class fell silent as he walked with his hands together under his chin, in a gesture of prayer. He looked at the ceiling and breathed loudly and soundly, as if concentrating on something that required all his physical and mental effort. He began to speak.

"Wittgenstein erases his own footprints with his last book, *Philosophical Investigations,* published after his death. His entire life has been a meditation on the *Tractatus* – a critical meditation. The only thing he cannot be accused of is a lack of critical rigor with himself: he is his most fearsome detractor. Truth is more important than his personal vanity, than his philosophical career which has demanded, in tribute, his whole life. The man lived like a Carthusian monk, and died like a martyr, sacrificing his entire philosophical life on the altar of truth."

Wise, next to me, was as usual taking notes at high speed. The sound of her pencil moving across the paper pervaded Frege's lecture with a crescendo of anxiety. No one spoke, no one laughed. An unpleasant oppression was growing in the environment. Frege's thoughts flowed on, with poetic and brilliant images rare in him who was always so precise and restrained.

"If Wittgenstein is correct, and we can talk only about what is verifiable, what we do with the theories of space and absolute time of Plato and Newton, or with the substance of Locke, or with necessity in causality and entelechy, which, according to certain Vitalists, explain organic life?"

The Adonis had delivered this sudden interrogatory in such an imperious voice that he interrupted Frege's lecture and left him speechless.

"How, in the end, do we explain the atom and certain situations in which elementary particles act as waves instead of particles?"

the Adonis continued, his voice booming louder and louder, rattling off postulates, syllogisms, science.

Frege, inexplicably, seemed to be losing the argument, not intellectually, because those of us who had gone to the library and studied the baseless objections to Logical Positivism knew the arguments discrediting what the Adonis was saying. But on the vital plane, in the attack of one life against another, the young man had the advantage. Frege tried, sadly, to raise the plane of conversation, to return to the intensity of philosophical rigor, but before that young audience, vibrating intensely in the immediate, he played a lamentable role.

Wise reached for the Adonis's hand under the desk and watched him admiringly, smiling with proud complicity.

Frege paled and grabbed his neck with his right hand.

"You! You have become deformed by Philosophy!" he cried out, his Austrian accent thicker than we had ever heard it, his face congested with anger.

As he said this he fell to the ground with a thud. His face, swollen and monstrously transformed by anger, began to relax. His features sharpened. His skin took on a transparent alabaster whiteness, and his lips spread, slowly, in a faint smile. Out of the right corner of his mouth a trickle of blood came snaking.

CONTAMINATED TELEPHONES

The middle-aged Irish woman with red hair and bulging green eyes took a cotton swab from her black satchel and stuck it into the pink cream. Her name, she said, was Aileen. She swirled the stick with flair and applied the substance to the mouthpiece of the telephone, a square, black dial instrument of the early 1960s.

"This will completely eliminate the microbes," she said with the officious tone of the evangelist. At that time, I could not speak much English, but I had taken comprehension classes on the Island, and understood exactly what she was saying.

Two very kind and polite old sisters, Ruth and Esther, the company's directors, were supervising Aileen as she showed me how to do the job. Early in the morning, before Aileen arrived, they had proudly explained all about the pink cream, the secret formula developed by their brother, Dr. Karl Klein, the company's president. After many unfruitful attempts, he had discovered a cream that eradicated tuberculosis bacilli on contact.

Dr. Klein emerged from the back room of his tiny office on the fourteenth floor of a building on Fifth Avenue. His white medical robe made me feel we had interrupted him while he was conducting an experiment that would lead to his next great breakthrough. This gave importance to his inviting me into his laboratory, where his entire purpose was to show me a slide under the microscope: creatures hidden inside what looked like a blue and purple marble floor, exactly like the photograph of the terrible Koch bacilli on the wall, witnessing our conversation of primarily enthusiastic smiles and nods.

"So, now you know that the cream is a great scientific discovery," said Ruth with sincere pride, after Dr. Klein said goodbye and disappeared back into his laboratory. "Our competitors tried to steal the formula, but we fought them in court and they didn't get away with it. Keep the jar with the cream well guarded. Last year more than 45,000 people caught tuberculosis by speaking on the telephone. Our secret formula not only cleans the telephones, it sterilizes them also."

I realized they were staging this entire demonstration because inexpensive young employees like me generally left very quickly.

Aileen's job this day was to take me around to several clients, show me how to clean telephones and relate to customers. On the reception room sofa were the satchels we'd need. Aileen packed her satchel methodically: first, the small iron cylinder that took the place of the receiver while we cleaned it, so it wouldn't ring busy if a call came in, then a bottle with white polishing liquid, then a buffing cloth. She left the jar of pink cream for last. Showing it to me, to my astonishment she whispered: "You won't have time to use this. Anyway, that story of the bugs is baloney. Do you believe Dr. Klein's for real? I think he's the family drunk and they keep him around for show. If you use this pink cream, you'll never finish. Just scoop out some cream from the jar every day, so when you turn in your satchel they won't suspect."

I looked at Aileen, mute. A lawyer I knew in San Juan had won a big case against the Puerto Rican telephone company by proving that contaminated mouthpieces had infected twenty operators with tuberculosis. Whether this pink cream worked or not, I couldn't say, because I didn't actually see it killing any bacilli under the microscope. Aileen was telling me not even to give it the benefit of the doubt.

Aileen and I arrived at 8 a.m. at the first on our list of clients, a millionaire in Rockefeller Center who, Aileen explained, had every nickel invested in the stock market. His was a big wood-paneled office, one wall of which took in Manhattan's grey sky behind the tops of big buildings. The millionaire was already at work, lounging on a caramel leather sofa while watching a Mickey Mouse cartoon and talking animatedly on the phone in heavily accented French.

Aileen whispered in my ear: "The stock market must be down. He's panicking." The millionaire, who seemed perfectly calm, hung up the phone, stood up, and said hello. He had a round red face and thinning blond hair, and wore wrinkled khakis and a cream-colored shirt. "Yet another new girl! What do you think of my office?" he asked cheerily.

After a few seconds of bewilderment, I opened my hands wide and said, "Big, *big*." He smiled, sat down, and turned his attention back to the cartoons. Aileen felt obliged to explain to the back of his head, "She understands, but speaks little English."

"She'll learn in a jiffy," the millionaire answered from the sofa without looking at her.

After cleaning his five telephones (one for each continent?), we moved on to five more offices in the building. We must have cleaned more than a hundred phones by a quarter to eleven, when Aileen announced we were finished. I had done most of the work and she had not allowed me to waste a minute using the pink cream. Rushing back to the office would raise the directors' suspicions, so she led me to a cafeteria and, to kill time, ordered two cups of coffee, which she paid for.

We sat in one of the booths lining both walls in the coffee shop on Lexington Avenue. Aileen took a metal flask from her purse and poured golden liquor that smelled like whiskey into her coffee.

"It's medicine," she said, looking guiltily at me while sipping the laced coffee. "How come you're working part-time? I am a middle-aged woman and I had to take this job, but you're young. You could get a full-time job somewhere."

I ransacked my small vocabulary for a reply. "Writer. Work morning, write afternoon."

Aileen sat back in shock. "A writer. What do you write about?"

I knew the perfect word because I had seen the magazine on all the newsstands. "*Life*," I answered proudly.

"Boy, that's a big subject!" said the woman without irony, gulping her coffee.

Ruth and Esther were in the reception room sitting in comfortable armchairs drinking tea and eating biscuits and cookies.

What could possibly make anybody think they were swindlers, those sweet old ladies with their abundant blue-white hair and stylish coiffures, their plump, cherubic cheeks, their welcoming smiles?

"How did she do?" asked Esther with enthusiasm.

"She did well. She'll be fine alone," said Aileen looking at me to be sure of her appraisal.

"Splendid!" exclaimed the sisters in chorus, clapping.

"Now, sit down and have tea with us," said Esther patting a place close to her on the sofa, while Aileen handed her satchel to Ruth and left. I envied Aileen and felt trapped. My English was not good enough to extricate myself gracefully, so I sat and smiled. "These are Austrian cookies, the best in the world," said Ruth, while Esther approved with enthusiastic nods. "We bought them at *die Konditorei*, hmm? the pastry shop on 86th Street?"

I could smell the delicate fragrance of vetiver coming from their underwear, reminding me of my grandmother. Somehow, I was not surprised to have tea with them on my first day of work, but was increasingly anxious to get home and start writing. The point of cleaning telephones was to be able to write, not to take tea with other foreigners, however much longer they had lived in New York.

Suddenly I found myself standing up. "Got to go. Got to *go*," I said slipping through the office glass door, giving them no time to speak and forgetting to leave my satchel.

In my little room in a ten-dollar-a week hotel on Upper Broadway – they charged prostitutes ten dollars an hour for the rooms but offered a better rate to the few "honest workers" – I sat in front of my tiny Olivetti typewriter hoping to write a play. Despite two Austrian cookies, I was hungry. Now I felt burdened to write something to justify taking a part-time job. I stared at the blank white page and saw rows of black telephones.

Somebody knocked. Juan, my neighbor, invited me to have stuffed grape leaves and Greek wine with him and his brother Luis. Juan, a short, thin young man with black eyes and black hair, and Luis, who had the body of Quasimodo and the most mischievous smile I have ever seen, had said hi to me in the hall a few times before. I accepted their invitation because I knew I was not going to be able to write. Juan explained the grape leaves by telling me they preferred Greek food to Puerto Rican and bought it at the little Greek stores on Ninth Avenue where they picked up Greek sailors.

I said I was writing a play. "Why do you write for the theater?" Juan asked, his mouth full of stuffed grape leaves.

"I like the theater because it makes me feel the work of fiction as palpable reality," I said in Spanish. "You can physically touch the characters embodied in the actors, and feel the raw emotion like lightning bolts paralyzing your heart."

What a relief to be able to speak in my mother tongue and sound like a normal person and not a moron. Spanish, I felt, was like breaking out of a prison of silence and shame.

"Wow," said Juan. "I can see you are a playwright. When I met you, I thought you were just trying to impress me."

The telephone rang and Juan answered it. After listening, he screamed at Luis: "We did it! We sold it!"

Luis undulated around the room like a belly dancer, his deformity making this victory lap intensely poignant. "We sold songs to Bobby Darin! We're rich!" he squealed. Lucky Nuyoricans, I thought, they know enough English to write songs for rock stars.

Juan danced over to the kitchenette, fished a bottle of cheap sparkling wine out of the mini-fridge and found three cups in the cabinet. Laughing, he popped the cork, his sallow face flushed.

Visions of their future artistic success made the three of us drunk on the cheap wine. I drifted over to the telephone and examined it carefully. A grey and black crust covered the earpiece and mouthpiece. I excused myself and went across the hall for my satchel. Like a magician I took out the jar with the pink cream and held it up for them to see, saying: "This will kill all the microbes on your mouthpiece." Then I cleaned their telephone with great care, holding it up tipsily to admire its intense shine. Juan and Luis watched me, astounded.

"Do you often clean phones when you visit people?" Juan asked.

I laughed. "I just got a part-time doing this." The brothers looked at each other as if I was obsessed. I ignored them and finished my task of protecting them from a horrible disease.

That week I worked hard. My part-time job turned full time because I insisted on using the pink cream. Aileen was right: there was no time to use it. I worked twice as long for the same pay and arrived home too tired to write a single word. The burden of writing paled by comparison with the weight of my new ethical responsibility to save people from tuberculosis – assuming the pink cream actually worked.

One morning, Aileen and I encountered each other as we picked up our satchels and job lists for the day. Aileen told me she had heard how late in the afternoon I returned the day before. I saw fear in her eyes because she thought I would accuse her. Why would I do that? It would be as bad as letting someone catch tuberculosis from a contaminated telephone. Her paycheck and her invalid husband's pitiful disability money were the only things keeping them off the street.

Friday came, and, tired and tormented as I was, I had my paycheck and was happy. I could eat a decent meal. I went to a cafeteria on Broadway to listen to the Jewish intellectuals. In Yiddish and English, they discussed literature, books, writers, and ideas, anything but the concentration camps many of them had survived. Some had long beards and wore black skullcaps acknowledging a superior being. They smelled of the naphthalene from the trunks and closets of the people who had donated their clothes. They were all dressed in black pants and jackets with white shirts, except for a woman named Rebecca, who always had on a discolored red velvet dress with a lace collar that once was beige or white, but had turned pink. She recited, in English and in a clear, soprano voice, insightful poems about life in the Polish ghetto. Everything about the cafeteria's clientele evoked East European pogroms, the war, an eternity of fear and poverty, but they mainly spoke of ideals and dreams. I felt comforted listening to these people and ate my plate of kosher meat loaf, mashed potatoes and carrots. It was expensive for my budget, but a delicious change from the canned macaroni and meatballs I lived on.

By Sunday morning, this warmth was gone and I was deeply depressed, a tree trying to grow with its roots in the air. The uplifting feeling produced by the conversation of the Jewish intellectuals and the other joyful experience of speaking Spanish with the Puerto Rican brothers, now excitedly planning futures as successful songwriters, contrasted sharply with the daily task I was facing. I woke up Sunday morning dreaming that the telephone cord was strangling me, maybe a flashback to my birth when I turned blue, strangled by the umbilical cord. All day Sunday, I lay in bed staring at the Olivetti on the desk a few feet away. Sunday night, I had nightmares about people dying of a new kind of cancer from talking on the phone while Dr. Klein frantically tried to formulate another pink cream to exterminate it.

On Monday, I was waiting at the door for Ruth and Esther to arrive. They were so pleased with my diligence that they gave me a brokerage firm on Wall Street as my only assignment. The elevator door opened on infinite rows of desks with black telephones, one of which was dimly ringing in the distance. I opened the glass door and ran to the desk. "Nobody here," I answered to stop the shrill ringing. "You are somebody," said a voice. "Tell Smith to sell. Sell. Sell. Sell!" he screamed. I hung up. Then all the telephones began to ring, each with a different tone. The apparatuses vibrated on the metal desks, demanding attention.

I ran around senselessly trying to answer them. "Nobody here. Nobody here. Nobody here.," I barked, and as soon as I hung up, more started to ring.

I observed myself from the ceiling as happens in dreams, in the middle of that big room, lighted by spectral fluorescent tubes and surrounded by row after row after row of ringing telephones. I saw myself opening my mouth wide to scream.

Leaning against the wall of the elevator, I let out a sigh of relief. I had to go home to think. On the subway, I noticed the satchel in my lap and realized that, somehow, I had to return it to the directors without letting them convince me to stay. I could see them offering me more tea and cookies and I would be lost. I trudged up the stairs to my room rehearsing possible excuses I could give to leave the job. I needed something out of the theater. A terrible fall. A fall so horrendous it would crush my leg and make it impossible for me to walk ever again. However, I had to walk there, to the office, so the fall would have to be serious enough to prevent me from working, but not from going this one time to see the sisters.

I ran to the drugstore downstairs and bought a roll of gauze. The next morning I wrapped the whole thing around my left leg and went to the office.

I had just come out of the subway near the New York Public Library when a woman started following me. I walked faster but finally she grabbed my arm. "May I help you cross the street? How did you do this to yourself? I'm a retired nurse, and I've never seen anybody with an injury as extensive as yours able to walk," she said.

"No time. Got to work. Got to work."

"I can't believe this sweatshop is forcing you to work with this injury. That's outrageous!"

The woman, middle-aged, stocky, her blond hair tied into a topknot over her rubicund peasant face, wrinkled into anger at the injustice I was suffering. Keeping pace with me, she said:

"I'm going with you and give them a piece of my mind."

"No. No. Don't understand. Got to go. Got to go!" I cried.

I removed the nurse's hand from my arm and ran from her misplaced compassion. The directors, surprised to see me, expressed alarm at my bandaged leg. They told me not to walk and Esther brought a chair. I sat and explained to them in English fragments that I had fallen down the stairs at the hotel.

"You can sue!" said Ruth.

Esther added, "We'll get you a lawyer."

"No. No. Can't work no more," I stopped them.

"At least file for disability. We'll fill out the forms for you," said Esther.

"No. Got to go. Great pain!"

Esther went to the back and brought some forms.

"Here. Fill them out when you feel better."

"Thank you. Thank you. Thank you!" I screamed.

I gave them my satchel and took the elevator down. Once on the sidewalk, I ran. I didn't care that the directors could be watching me from the office window, or a nurse, doctor, or orthopedic surgeon might see me. I ran like hell and the gauze trailed after me like a tail.

THE EYES OF OLORÚN

They say that everything in the land of Uzú changed when Efi, king of Ifá, came very early one morning, at the song of the rooster, to ask permission to visit the sacred forest. His earth-colored skin gleaming with that steel glow distinctive of the men of Ifá, his eyes green as a sea whose shore has its sand at great depth, Efi had stripped off his royal robe, yellow as the rising Sun, and had donned rags to signal his penance.

Efi carried with him the royal board called the wing of the Koré, a wooden plank carved from a tree of the sacred forest. It was covered in geometric drawings that had magical power, and crowned with the eye of Olorún (the one who transforms), an enormous emerald by which Olorún wounds the unjust and the wicked with the light of the Sun and the crushing pressure of Pelu Tolo, the invisible star of the tenth moon that revolves around the Tiger Star in the constellation of the Beetle. The wing of the Koré was sheathed in leather to protect it from the affront of human glances and the agitation of light. Efi had brought it for the religious ceremony he would have to perform in honor of his royal ancestors, to engage their help before entering into combat with the buffalo-men who were ravaging Ifá – setting fire to its circular huts, stealing its cattle, raping its women. Efi was the greatest and most handsome warrior ever born in the lands of the Bambaras and, despite his youth, his fame had spread far and wide thanks to Ifá's old men, who told war stories by firelight at the banquets and great tribal ceremonies.

Before the coming of Efi, Uzú had been under the spell of a sorceress called Lamai. She had arrived at the village as a child ten years before, accompanied by an old man who claimed to have rescued her from the buffalo-men who had destroyed the place where she lived. Soon the people came to know the girl's great powers: she could paralyze animals and men at will. But her magical words also protected the people from natural disasters caused by wind, rain or the overflow of the river, as well as those caused by man, such as war.

The people built a wooden palace for Lamai in the center of Uzú and brought her their best offerings of animals and fruits of the land. Upon reaching adolescence, Lamai was surprised to see an image in the crystal-clear waters of the river. At first, because she had never seen a more beautiful woman, she thought she was seeing the goddess of the waters, but when she made some gestures that the reflection of the river imitated, she understood that she was seeing herself. From that moment, Lamai began to demand that the people bring her gold to adorn that body and that face, and make her seem even more beautiful.

By the time foreigners came hunting for souls to work in distant lands, Lamai had come to feel very profoundly the attraction of gold.

"Hear me, you crocodiles," she told the visitors with contempt, "you may take away only those who accidentally pass through the Path of Sorrows, because they have offered themselves as victims for sacrifice. I alone will know where that path is and I myself will never send anyone to it. Whoever goes there will have been judged by Olorún."

Taking a deep breath, she added: "So, hang your nets to catch the wingless fish that know not how to escape. You will owe me gold for each one, not feathers or seeds – pure gold in earrings, bracelets, and necklaces."

Along with the love of gold, Lamai became possessed by the thrill of making a laughing stock of men. She delighted in seducing the proudest of warriors, so that afterwards she could trick them into new schemes she would dream up.

Just then Efi, king of Ifá, arrived, asking permission to enter the sacred forest that had been in the safe keeping of the kings of Uzú since the time of Nommo, the man-fish who had fertilized the Earth to create the six pairs of twins that had brought forth the human race.

When Efi entered the palace of Uzú with all the humility of a supplicant, Lamai could not stop looking at the green of his eyes, which provoked in her a strange fascination.

She knew she ought to give Efi everything he asked, but a strange obstinacy possessed her. She had always given permission to outsiders to visit the sacred forest, but this case was different.

"I do not grant favors to any man whose body has not previously offered me homage," she said haughtily.

"Great Queen, the bee's destiny is to visit the most beautiful flowers, but the King must choose. My ancestors are waiting in the sacred forest, with their white faces, for me to bring them the wing of the Koré and take them out of the world of that pause where no noise or color reaches. My body does not matter. My people are dying every day."

Lamai gestured with her chin to one of her guards, and he ordered two others to escort Efi. They left the palace leading the king, who assumed he was being escorted to the sacred forest until, after an interval, the guards turned on him. Efi threw the wing of the Koré and, at once, it became indistinguishable from other fallen trees in the forest. The guards bound Efi's hands and feet, dragged him to a mound of earth, and covered his body with honey. Efi did not know why they had done this until he felt the ants tickling his back.

The next morning, Efi's unconscious body was swollen and made almost unrecognizable by the bites of ants that had tortured him all night long. He was discovered by Ifá guards who had come looking for him. They carried him home to his palace and applied a yellow cream to his skin, then covered it with many leaves.

The people of Ifá organized a drum vigil to beg Olorún for the recovery of their king, still unconscious and prey to strange dreams. Efi saw Lamai in her palace, unable to think about anything but him. She threw the snail-shells of divination to know where he was, and then filled a basin of water to view the reflection of his swollen body on the bed. Lamai saw Efi's green eyes everywhere and, raving mad, paced through her palace that was crammed with gold bracelets, anklets, earrings, and collars flung in every corner.

After some time, Efi woke up, cured, and asked about the buffalo-men: was the town now free of them? His men told him they feared an attack at any moment because the enemy had heard the king was ill. At once, Efi devoted himself to organizing battle simulations to prepare his warriors, and to strengthening the fortifications.

The buffalo-men attacked one day at dawn and the Ifá warriors gave battle. When the struggle reached its peak, Efi froze just as he was about to slash an enemy in the ribs. Seeing Efi paralyzed, the buffalo-men hurled their spears, but Efi remained standing on the sand as if he were still alive. His wounds opened like mouths and sucked the spears deep into his body, spilling not a single drop of blood. The buffalo-men recognized at once that they were witnessing sorcery and ran away in terror, never to return to that bewitched town. Efi was still standing, pierced by spears, his skin fresh, alive, covered in sweat.

The people of Ifá respectfully approached their king. They brought him fruits and vegetables as a sign of adoration and surrounded him singing in low voices the songs of Olorún and the god of war.

Watching all this reflected in the water of her basin, Lamai burst into laments, screams, howls. Until that moment she had wanted to tear this man apart with her own hands, but when she saw him slaughtered by her spell, she felt an unbearable, animal pain. She shouted all night long, shaking the locks of her hair, while the people of Uzú watched and waited outside the palace.

The next morning, instead of a young woman in the prime of youth and beauty, a stooped old woman with white hair emerged dressed in the robes of Lamai. She brought as much of her gold as she could carry in a basket and handed it out to everyone she encountered. When she had disposed of this precious jewelry, she began to remove her garments, one by one, dropping them on the sand. The entire town was following her and saw a wrinkled crone with flaccid, pendulous breasts step into the river, crying out to see green eyes in the water. Soon her body disappeared downstream.

Upon accidentally returning by the Path of Sorrows, the people of Uzú fell into the nets that the men with the pink faces of pigs had put up in the forest to ensnare and carry them off into slavery.

THE BLUE JAR FROM DAMASCUS

I

Monotonously, rhythmically, José's foot moved on the kick wheel that operated the turntable where the work was taking shape. With one wet palm cupped around the solid orb of kaolin and feldspar, he pressed forcefully down and out with the blade of his other hand as his foot kept the turntable rotating. As if by a miracle, the thrown clay grew tall and shapely and, after making sure the interior was as smooth as the exterior, he lifted it gently into the kiln.

Now, dipping a hand into the mixture of copper oxide and alkali glaze, he assessed its consistency between his thumb and index finger, squeezing it, willing the substances in it to unite in such a way that one specific color, the blue of a clear winter sky, the sea on a calm summer day...the blue eye of God...would come into being. He rinsed his hands in a bowl of cool water and began to stir, but not beat, the glaze.

On the morrow, he would glaze the now cooled jar for the second firing. First, he would inspect the vessel for flaws, holding it up to the light, turning it gently with the pride a father might lavish on a new son. Then, when he was certain of its body's flawlessness, he would coat its curves with the viscosity of this latest iteration of the blue glaze. This process created in the skin of his fingers the tender feeling of a love game, which would spread to his whole body. At last, he would fire the jar in the kiln at its hottest, immolate it to the point where, his hope become out-and-out desire, the glaze would be transmuted into that perfect blue.

Then, as always for him, the tactile enjoyment of creation was invaded by pain: a dull, shooting pain that had haunted him since that day more than twenty years before when he had encountered the blue porcelain jar for the first time.

On that occasion, he had accompanied his father, one of the most famous potters in Cordoba, to visit Abd al-Rahman III, head of the Umayyad dynasty, who had just proclaimed himself caliph, successor of the prophet Muhammad, Defender of the Faith, in addition to being Amir al-Mu'minin, prince of believers. The caliph wanted to share his moment of triumph with his favorite potter and had invited him to his palace. José remembered the intense black dye, like a raven's wing, that Abd al-Rahman III used to color his blond hair, inherited along with his deep blue eyes from two Christian princesses, and also his magnificence and boundless beauty. It was on that occasion that José saw the ruler's imposing figure and surroundings, the overwhelming awe produced by this personification of power and oriental luxury, as manifest in a single object: a porcelain jar of the most intense blue he had ever seen, which the Umayyad ruler had on that occasion proudly displayed to his father.

The jar had been precious to the caliph's ancestor, the emir Abd al-Rahman I, called the Fair and also the Righteous One, who had brought the Umayyad dynasty to Cordoba. The artefact was one of the few cherished objects that had been salvaged from the palace in Damascus during the family's escape from the descendants of Muhammad's uncle Abbas and the other usurpers who toppled the rightful Umayyad dynasty in 750. In the escape, no sooner had Abd al-Rahman I gotten across the Euphrates with a few belongings, than he had watched his younger brother swim back into enemy hands and, instead of being welcomed in surrender, he had his head chopped off by an Abbasid scimitar.

On the occasion of José's father's visit, Abd al-Rahman III had brought the jar from the palace treasury room to remind himself of the first Abd al-Rahman, and also to proclaim that by elevating himself over his ancestors, who had only dared call themselves emirs – one who gives the orders, tribal chief – he had restored the Umayyad family's legitimacy as the leaders of Islam – as caliphs.

That visit as a boy had inspired José to become a famous potter like his father, whom the caliph had treated as an equal. During his apprenticeship, until his father's death, José dedicated his free time to producing the caliph's jar's precise shade of blue, which seemed to embody the joyful, clear sky of Cordoba within its exquisitely translucent, diamantine glaze.

When José became master, everything else ceased to matter. He created numberless exquisitely beautiful porcelain pieces, from which he had earned a modest fortune – and still he had not achieved the proper suspension of copper oxide, or discovered any alternate substance, to create a jar like the one that obsessed him.

At the end of the day, he again grumbled that his latest work no doubt again would proclaim his failure. Fatima, his wife, decided she had to speak.

Despite being named for the Prophet Mohammed's daughter, Fatima was a descendant of Romans and Visigoths. She was born Christian but converted to Islam – was a *maula*, as the Arabs called converts – while José was Mozarabic, a faithful Christian. Despite their differences of belief, the childless couple got along well, and he continued to be esteemed for his artisanal talents, treated with the same great respect as José's father and grandfather by the Umayyads from the time when that great family came to al Andalus, and religious persecution faded away.

"Why don't you visit the Caliph and propose to buy the jar?" was what Fatima suggested. "You're rich, you can offer the Caliph a respectable sum. True, he's the richest ruler in all of Islam, but he's also a fervent believer – maybe he will take pity on you."

José thought this was the most ridiculous suggestion he had heard in his entire life. Had his wife lost her mind? He might be a Christian, but he knew his Umayyad history.

He knew the story of the beautiful slave who had turned away when the Caliph went to kiss her during an orgy: as punishment for her effrontery, he told his eunuchs to burn her face with a torch. Also, at his right hand the Caliph kept an executioner armed with a scimitar. This terrifying personage stood on a leather mat to protect the rich carpets from bloodstains that might add to the prince's displeasure.

It was even said that the Caliph had joined his courtiers to watch the execution of his rebellious son, Abd Allah, and was much amused by the startled horror reflected in the eyes of the young man's severed head.

Against all common sense, José accepted his wife's advice because he could not continue living with that constant feeling of abject failure. On a sunny morning filled with the twitter of birds, feeling more self-assured than usual, the potter made up his mind to seek an audience with the Caliph, and offer to buy the blue jar.

II

More than twenty years had passed since José's visit as a child. In the interim Abd al-Rahman III had left the Alcazar of Cordoba for the palatial city (really, the city-palace) of Madinat al-Zahra, the City of the Flower, which the Caliph had built on the outskirts of Cordoba to rival in splendor the city of Damascus, still in the hands of the Abbasids. He had given himself a new title: Al-Nasir Li Din-Allah, meaning servant of the Merciful, he who fights victoriously for the religion of Allah, which the people had reduced to Al-Nasir – the Victorious, reflecting his numberless successes in war. José in Cordoba had heard again and again of the magnificence of Madinat al-Zahra, of its four thousand columns of marble and onyx brought from all the corners of the Earth, of its hundred copper-plated doors, of its Hall of the Caliphs with sixteen doors with ebony-and-ivory frames supported by pillars of crystal, and the fountain of mercury that, like melted silver, gushed out of a spout made of porphyry. All this made José feel fear. He was certain that the sovereign would try to dazzle him with the luxury of his empire, his will of iron that had brought Visigothic Toledo to its knees, his alliance of equals with the Christian emperor in Byzantium.

José arrived at the palace trying not to think about what was around him. Wandering uncomfortably among the richly attired courtiers, in no time he was convinced that he had made a terrible mistake. Now, how happy he would be to wake up in his own bed and remember this luxury as just a dream, instead of being in the midst of it, the coffered cedar ceilings, the marble columns, the onyx tracery, all of it. His legs trembled at the thought that he was soon to be in the presence of this Muslim potentate who, arrogantly stroking his jeweled scimitar, delighting in his visitor's abject terror, would fuel the thought that José's temerity would end in his being decapitated. He rebuked himself for stupidly having listened to his wife, for insanely having believed the Caliph would ever consider selling him the jar, for arrogantly dreaming that a common potter could make such a proposition to a force of nature whose audacity and intelligence had fascinated entire populations, bent them to his will, and revived the Umayyad caliphate.

Eunuchs guided José through halls with gold-plated walls and ceilings that reflected their shapes in a golden blur as they walked, until finally they emerged in the sunlight of a simple courtyard with a floor of tamped sand. There, the potter saw a peasant in a rustic cloth tunic, seated cross-legged on a humble reed mat. This, one of the eunuchs informed him, was al-Nasir, the Victorious.

You are making fun of me, José almost said out loud. He decided to maintain his dignity in the face of this impostor.

"I have asked to speak with the Caliph," José said haughtily.

"You are speaking with the Caliph, my son. More than twenty years have passed since you visited me with your father, whom I will always remember with affection, because of the beauty of his pottery that lightened the burdens of my heart. Then, I was young and felt the passion for war, the joy of victory, the satisfaction of knowledge, and the pleasure of love and the arts. My passions have aged me far worse than Time."

José glanced at the eunuchs surrounding them, armed with scimitars, garbed in white tunics under gleaming bronze cuirasses. They were not laughing at the humble man's witticism. "How can this man be the great Caliph?" he asked the guards.

The man on the mat made an almost imperceptible gesture, and the eunuchs retreated into the opulent palace.

"Now that we are alone, my son, you will not feel ill at ease in the presence of my guards."

"I've come to see the Caliph to offer to purchase the blue jar."

"The blue jar?"

"Yes, a porcelain jar I saw in the Alcazar of Cordoba over twenty years ago. Since then I have worked to the exclusion of all else to be able to reproduce the indescribable blue and the iridescent transparency of that jar. I have never been able to replicate it. But in trying, I have created ceramic pieces that have become famous, not as great as my father's, not perhaps deserving to be in the palace of the Caliph, but respectable enough for me to charge good money for them. And," he added belligerently, "I am willing to give everything I own for that jar. Since I can't duplicate it, at least the original would be mine."

The man seemed to weigh seriously the words spoken by José, and looked at him with some tenderness.

"My son, let me suggest that you spend a few days with me as a guest here in my house. Later we will talk about the jar."

III

That night José was attended in great splendor by eunuchs dressed in colorful attire, and as the Qur'an would say, by "nubile damsels resembling hyacinths and coral." These women of heavenly beauty, dressed in Persian silks fastened with ornaments of gold thread, would promptly serve anything it crossed José's mind to ask for. Although José thought the farce went on far too long, he kept arrogantly asking for whatever came into his head, vaguely suspecting the delicacies might be poisoned. The unseen Caliph might want not just to subject him to ridicule, but also to kill him, as an amusement for his courtiers. However, hunger always won out over prudence, and he tasted every single dish they brought.

At dinner's end, the young women took him to a luxurious room scented with musk and gray amber. They gave him to understand, between kisses and caresses, that he could choose from among them a companion with whom to while away the hours of the night. But José was afraid they would attack him while he slept, and told them that by preference he always slept alone.

He had trouble drifting off, as he indignantly considered the Caliph's perfidy: why was he setting such traps for him? Probably the room had hidden spyholes through which the ruler and his depraved courtiers could watch, amused, as a rustic potter tried to make love to divine nymphs, the Caliph's alabaster courtesans with whom he satisfied his gluttonous lust. It was said that the Caliph had more than six thousand women, changing them every night; also, that he was no stranger to young men, or even to orgies involving animals. Jaded by these foul pleasures, the potter thought, the Caliph had now descended to the truly base pastime of spying on his lowly subjects in bed.

The next day was taken up with pampering by slaves and annoying conversations with the bogus caliph. The blue jar was never mentioned. When night came, the lavish dinner was reprised, this time served by beautiful ephebes. José had never seen such beauty in male faces and bodies. Their perfection was such that they surpassed the beauty of any woman he had ever seen, including his wife in her youth, perhaps because these young men also had the gallantry and superb bearing of the stronger sex. José contemplated with rancor that the Caliph had spent his life enjoying Paradise, while he had been wasting his life trying to replicate the blue porcelain jar of the Umayyads.

Anticipating their offer, José told the young men that he preferred to sleep alone.

The third day was another repetition of the banquet, except that now the dinner was served by children of both sexes who, at the end of the feast, made the same suggestions as the women of the first night and the ephebes of the second. Exasperated, José was furious because they were infants and he rejected them with a shove. This was rock bottom. He decided that in the morning he must unmask the man dressed as a peasant and demand that the true Caliph show himself so he could tell him what he thought of him, even at the risk of being beheaded.

Very early the next morning there was a knock on the bedroom door, while José was still asleep. A eunuch told him that al-Nasir would like to see him in the Hall of the Caliphs. José dressed in haste and, furiously trying to think what scathing things he could say about the cynical torments he had been subjected to, he went to meet the sovereign.

Dressed in a ceremonial *thobe* of fine white silk adorned with pearls, diamonds, and rubies, seated on a lush prayer rug, there, in the Hall of the Caliphs, was the peasant caliph-impersonator who had annoyed the potter so during the past few days. In his fine hand he held a rose – no, actually the rose was *at rest* in his hand – a pink rose. Now, for the first time, the potter noticed the piercing dark blue eyes of the prince whom he and his father had visited two decades before. "My son, during these days when you have been my guest," he said, "I have seen you repeatedly reject the rewards of Paradise on earth. You have been a model of prudence and restraint. At all times you have behaved with modesty and devotion. You have listened to me in silence and I have been able, in the course of these three days, to have a true friend. For all the pleasure your visit has given me, I reward you with this."

He raised the pink rose and pointed with it to the blue jar of Damascus, placed to his right on a brocaded tapestry.

José looked at al-Nasir's smiling face, his perfect white teeth that age had failed to stain, his broad and pellucid face, his clear, kind look, where the shining star of generosity resided.

José abruptly turned and ran. Without the blue jar, without looking back, he flew, until the superb minaret of the mosque of Madinat al-Zahra, where the muezzin had begun to chant the adhan, seemed but a mirage lost in the distance.

ENCOUNTERS IN THE CHAPEL

Confronted by those immortal creatures, one senses that one lacks the right to exist, as if the blood flowing through one's veins is a worthless liquid destined to feed useless things, mere ephemera. It's not because those creatures put on airs of importance – it has nothing to do with their infernal pride (clearly, they are well aware of this). It's just something intrinsic to their natures. They are beings so vital and, as it seems, simultaneously so devoid of outward-directed anger, that their presence always makes me shed cold tears of tenderness.

When I first became aware of the existence of these delicious creatures, it was as if a ray of light had penetrated the regions of my consciousness and caused it to vibrate, as if I were just about to enter a radiant puberty of spirit. I was recumbent before the high altar, caressing the beads of my silver rosary, which had been given a special blessing by the Holy Father in the most recent Year of the Eucharist. I was lost in the joyful mysteries, murmuring Hail Marys, dozing off thanks to the luxuriant scent of the gladioli I'd brought as an offering to the Virgin. Glancing to my side, almost exactly to the right of my habit, despite the gloom that reigned in the chapel, I could make out their graceful figures, undeterred by the timid blinking of the candles.

The creatures were reclining, not in prayer, but rather lying down and making grimaces in the direction of the tabernacle, which housed that day's supply of communion wafers. As to their appearances – their physical features and manner of attire – they seemed perfectly natural. Only their telltale smiles and sparkling glances, which pierced through all the living or inanimate things around them, gave them away. Then, one of them sneaked up on me, stood there, and, to my utter surprise, started stroking my breasts. I had no idea how to react, given that this act was in no way permitted by my order's rules of chastity. But rebelling would have indicated that I tacitly accepted the existence of these beings, contrary to teachings promulgated hundreds of years ago at the Council of Trent. No other solution occurred to me except to put more passion into my prayers, begging the Virgin to intercede and cast out the temptation that lurked in those incredibly agile hands.

Contrary to this, my ardent wish, nothing happened. The Virgin was still on the altar, virtually covered in white gladioli and disfigured by the flickering light of the candles. All of a sudden, the creatures burst out laughing and began slapping one another on the buttocks, which appeared to cause them even more of this appalling hilarity. I noted that they were engaged in certain activities, preposterous when one considered that we were in a chapel. One of the taller ones was applying pink enamel to his toenails; another combed her hair fussily and flirted with her figure reflected in the mirror of a powder compact; a couple had created a chair out of their intertwined arms and wandered around carrying a chubby-cheeked fat boy who had the letters INRI stuck to his forehead. My neighbor got tired of fondling my breasts and was now entertaining himself by searching for my navel under my habit. As we must don, according to our order's requirements, a very stiff linen petticoat, more like a girdle, it was quite difficult for him to find anything. He even seemed to be getting a little desperate. But then, impervious to my distress, he removed my coif, wimple, and veil, followed by my starched white guimpe and the image pinned to it, the Sacred Heart of Mary with the motto of our order, "Sacred Heart of Mary, be my salvation." In short order, and with great deftness, he undressed me. I let him do it because I thought it was a test: God would repeat the story of Abraham and Isaac. Doubtless, He was waiting for things to reach their climactic moment to send His heavenly armies to my aid. He would not let me succumb to the lust of these depraved – albeit immensely persuasive – beings.

It is true that, notwithstanding my well-established piety and authentic vocation, I have always kept up my profound interest in secular philosophy. This penchant for the worldly has earned me many reproaches from my superiors as well as the inevitable sanctimonious contempt from the other sisters. This predilection I mention clearly must have sown some evil ideas in my conscience: I reasoned that, since heavenly armies had not come to my aid, something highly significant had been revealed to me. If I succumbed to the lechery of ethereal beings, this was a sign that God had neglected to make us strong in the face of wiles beyond the power of our defenses. This signified that Thomism, which said divine law took precedence over natural law, hinged on a relative and debatable point. Otherwise, how could Thomism be justified when we are presented with insurmountable evidence negating it? I had no way to stop those hands that undressed me: they did not exist. They could touch me: there was no way for me to touch them. My hands passed through their bodies. This clearly eclipsed reason, but manifestly was happening. My skin was a reliable witness, shuddering as it did under the caresses of those incubi and succubae. Possibly my vocation was never as sound as it should have been, since my nature always had a certain propensity to revel in the senses. It never occurred to me to conceal my irrepressible wanton nature, which the brush of another's skin woke up to sensual pleasures with extraordinary force.

Clearly, no one was hastening to my aid. I made up my mind to surrender to the situation; bodies tend not to contain themselves in certain climactic moments.

I rejoiced in those beings of light, of a beauty beyond my power of evocation and description.

I came to confuse purely sexual pleasures with a joyful ascent of the soul. I knew about love in the infinite range of its manifestations. We tried out all possible delicacies on the human and immaterial scales. The candles' light cast sharp reflections that sparkled on our sweat-covered skins. On the great vault above the high altar, the painted angels gawked with stunned and delighted expressions at our dance of the senses. Sometimes, the bench would rock with great booming noises, convulsing the chapel air with sacred vibrations. At the end of our salacious ardor, perspiring and panting, I understood the similarity of soul and body. The memory of those moments did not leave me for days. In the refectory, in the dark halls, and even in the harsh austerity of my cell, the image of those crystalline beings would suddenly start from my memory. It was not long before I returned to the chapel, at the same hour, with the same number of candles and the obligatory white gladioli. Our meetings have been transformed into an anticipation of Heaven.

SEMPRE CONTIGO

When Ixte comes toward me I jump up as if shocked by high-voltage currents that make me convulse in spasms. My body stops being mine. My reactions defy understanding – my emotions, movements, thoughts non-existent, as if I were on a roller-coaster.

I'm not the only one who feels this way. Ixte affects – actually, electrifies and manipulates at will – the entire group I belong to, the Paris Club. Ixte's biggest thrill is to destroy others' defenses – to triumph in that physical siege of emanations launched by an ultra-sexual body. Ixte kills with a glance and revives with smiles. You can survive as an individual until you get close; then, Ixte reels you in, and you find yourself orbiting and revolving to the rhythm of light.

I've never orbited around anyone. I have looked, non-stop, for ways to define myself when facing Death, rid myself of that fear that turns most people into jelly. I have never caved with Death in view.

That said, Ixte is an animal I cannot face without trembling.

And now I pursue this tremor as if it were a drug. When my body shakes, life attains an intensity that makes everything transcendent. Words develop so much weight they take on a life of their own, revealing their many meanings, pass through echo chambers where we, terrified, hear the true words of the Being, words that create us as easily as they destroy us.

Ixte's body is purely classical, face geometrically perfect. A keen student of beauty in art, Ixte seems to have incorporated this and turned it into a right of first night. That explosive vitality injects something violent into this harmonic classicism, something savage, animal: feral green eyes glowing with the intensity of a jungle creature at night, absolute, desperate, rapacious ways of making love.

This level of exaggerated predation is something Ixte builds with different levels of imaginativeness around a persona, fruit of an inner eroticism created unwillingly. If a heart thirsts for fulfillment and longs for infinite horizons, Ixte turns into its black hole.

II

Now we find ourselves face to face in a piano bar. The meeting is apparently fortuitous, but nothing is accidental with Ixte. I can study that face receiving me with a friendly, welcoming expression. If that face's beauty were its only fascination, everything would be so simple. But beauty is the least complex of Ixte's devious diversions.

Ixte smiles and we sit at the piano bar that's pulsating with chords of a romantic jazz piece.

"This is so bizarre! You! The last person I was hoping to find...." From Ixte's lips, the insult is somehow praise.

Aware what a privilege it is to run into Ixte in reality, not just in dreams or memories, my senses sharpen, tune in at peak awareness to bask in the splendor of this being, make sure that every particular of this moment is cherished, savored, voraciously devoured.

The glut of details rushing into my brain plunges me into utter stupidity, a state Ixte is no stranger to and, moreover, subtly despises.

Abruptly Ixte pushes back the chair and stands, thighs tense inside tight pants. The sun-bronzed torso under a gossamer-thin shirt of fine white cotton disappears among the dancers and shortly returns with two drinks, one set down in front of me and the other raised to those lips, savoring the liquor. It's typical of Ixte not to ask what you want and bring just exactly what you were thirsting for.

I down the drink in one swallow and study the dance floor. Ixte rises and leads the charge through the crowd. Jazz morphs into an old Brazilian song the pianist croons, turning it into a sensual caress.

Ixte dances violently. The dancers make space.

My own dance is no match for this intoxicated rapture with life, these orgiastic vibrations of Love and Sex. I'm terrified that I'm going to wake up in bed from a dream about this dance and this piano bar – but this is reality. We are dancing. I'm lost in those green eyes and my skin feels the sweat pouring off those temples.

The music becomes hypnotic – *Sempre contigo, sempre contigo* – With you forever, forever with you, the singer serenades in Portuguese. The speakers project the deep voice at the walls, the walls catch the sound, it bounces back and forth.

Behind Ixte a figure materializes, gripping some shiny thing. Despite the dim light, I recognize a Paris Club face as the figure mechanically edges closer. Under the red reflector illuminating us from the ceiling, the silvery shape crystallizes into a gun.

I can understand the implacable obsession of the creature pointing a revolver at Ixte's back and even feel compassion. I search for the green of Ixte's eyes when the shot rings out, watch that green gradually giving way to the black of dilated pupils. My only fear is that this demented bullet Love is hurling at us will be stopped by one of Ixte's ribs. Ardent relief comes when the missile boring through Ixte explodes in my torso. I have no time to regret that our dance didn't end in an erotic romp in bed. I pity the person who shot us because I know that only loneliness awaits until the end of days. Loneliness, and memories of Ixte.

I collapse, carrying Ixte with me, and cling to the green of those eyes until, powerless to escape, I'm engulfed by the vast blackness of those expanding pupils that draw me, with one stroke, into the abyss.

APPARITION OF THE GODDESS

Because everything now can easily be put in the hollow of one's hand, even squeezed down to infinitesimal size, so too can we reduce this dark premonition, convert it into something small, unessential, even portable. This premonition is the mirror of the goddess, or rather, the force through which her essence manifests itself. Putting worship in your hand, that sharp jolt that flattens your chest when she begins her walk through the mountains, reducing *that* to a mathematical formula, would be worse than sacrilegious – it would be stupid. Having said that, I gladly offer to put some order to this confused mess of feelings; and yes, I am capable of classifying them in an organized and single-minded way. Such a high margin of error exists that this investigation must be carried out meticulously. I will begin by trying to determine the essence of the goddess, or, more simply, by explaining my terminology, that is, what I understand by the equivocal, little-used word "goddess." And yes, I can answer questions without being shocked or getting angry. Her divine powers are intrinsic to her nature – and that's not a play on words intended to confuse the gullible. What I understand by "divine" is everything that is beyond the human, beyond its possibilities. To support my thesis, I offer several valid arguments. One is the divine's patent ability to pass through objects, to fly, to take on proteic form in an infinite number of dissimilar appearances. Frequently, just to give a random example, she decides to manifest as a flower – not just any flower, but a gigantic blossom exploding with colors and emanating rare fragrances. When this happens, the sky turns into a pane of transparent blue glass, divided by bands and tame clouds gently floating north. Then the fireworks and dances start, and her utterances reach us in a thousand different languages. And she can be mistaken for a scimitar, but she also takes the form of a peacock, yet when she dives into the ocean, she covers herself entirely with scales of an incandescent purple that glow beneath the light of the stars. The intent of the goddess's epiphanies is impenetrable to me, since she has never referred to it, and I find it difficult to deduce using our atrophied laws of logic. Instead, she generally speaks of unknown planets and regions, and genuinely enjoys giving sensory descriptions of the places she names. She uses metaphor repeatedly (and sometimes imperfectly) – but her imagination (or her descriptive power) is remarkable, and the musical tone of her voice is also praiseworthy. As for her beauty, it is imponderable: her eyes are dark abysses, incandescent universes where everything is in full bloom. I would venture to say, though, that her legs are a little skinny in proportion to the rest of her body, and that her feet are rather large. Apart from all this data, I should add that she has a problematic interest in warriors and everything having to do with war – yet am not convinced that Pallas Athena is her true identity. I cannot say that she resembles her, nor does her figure suggest to me anything like the goddess of wisdom. I'd rather leave that point on hold, in the absence of conclusive evidence. Rather, she suggests love to me, even though I don't think she's Aphrodite, because she's not particularly plump. All I can say is that her apparitions have upset my existence, just as Pluto disrupts the orbit of Uranus. Also, I tend to expect her when night falls and the sea turns into a gelatinous animal that guards transcendent secrets. Then I light my bonfire with the requisite aromatic herbs, set three porous stones in the shape of an equilateral triangle with the tip facing south, and utter the supreme word. The goddess does not delay in appearing, with her thousand different faces, her thousand colors of skin, showing off her divine attributes, her infinite splendor. Who can sleep on those terrifying nights when she delivers vibrant words that penetrate like a tiger's teeth! What human eye would not tremble at the sacred black door that she opens without hesitation, without letting loose her veils or her laughter! And her love is like twisting in a bed of thorns, like throwing oneself into an abyss of darkness where there is never an end. All I can say is that the object of all this is totally beyond my ability to understand.

Doubtless, all this could fit in one hand, could be condensed and explained by qualified technologists. Yes, they could do exactly as they have done with the Sun, which now fits in a single word.

HEADS IN THE SAND

The man opened his mouth wide, to make sure the torrential rain fell on his tongue. Had he not been afraid of drowning, he would have started singing when the downpour cascaded into his sand-paper-parched throat. At some point in the past two days, the raging Antillean Sun had suddenly hidden itself behind black and gray clouds, and only after what seemed like a month, the storm had moved on, dragging away its howling winds, its tremendous explosions of lemon-colored lightning, its loud, stony cracks of thunder that sounded like mountains smashing together – all, at last, reduced to feeble grumbling.

His thirst quenched, the man lowered his head to keep the still-torrential rain out of his eyes and nostrils. The desperate feeling that comes from nearly drowning gave way to a tentative sensation of well-being, then of curiosity, as he peered in the dim light at what was over there on his right. In looking, he tried to turn his torso, but was stopped by the sand tightly compacted around his entire body.

Three or so yards away, the head of a young woman was barely visible. Her extremely white skin and short black hair seemed familiar, as did her mouth, which she opened to suck in the raindrops. Farther off, at about six yards, was a boy, maybe five years old, also buried, all but his head. This he inclined forward, seemingly asleep. The boy's position was not on a line with the man and the woman, who were about equidistant from the water's edge, which was distinguishable by whitish bands of thundering surf. Much closer to the sea, the boy's relative position reminded the man of the star Mintaka, offset a bit from the axis of two other stars, Alnitak and Alnilam, the three that make up Orion's belt. The man smiled when he realized that at this critical moment, he could call up his astronomy.

"Wake the boy and tell him to lift his head and drink!" he shouted at the woman, concerned that the still-howling gusts of wind would steal his words.

The woman closed her mouth and turned her head to the left to look at the man. Even in the half-light, her large, bright blue eyes had the transparency and brilliance of jewels.

Then she turned and called out in a beautiful soprano voice: "Wake up, boy! Drink the rainwater!" The boy shook back the wet black hair clinging to his forehead and, eyes still closed, opened his mouth towards the gray sky.

The rain stopped, the clouds parted, the wind abated. The sand that imprisoned the man's body seemed to be drying out and its humid cold receding. Not to have that rain lashing at his head and eyes and his hair constantly dripping water was a relief. But now, the sweet, acid smell of dead fish snagged in mangrove roots and branches was beginning to nauseate him.

To the left, the beach was empty, at least as far as he could tell. The delicate Sun of the first post-storm morning appeared on the horizon from behind an enormous white cumulus cloud.

As soon as the Sun's rays touched the man's face, the sand began to glitter like diamonds. This produced another burst of emotion in his chest: the sparkle was coming from thousands of tiny transparent crabs whose shells acted like mirrors reflecting the light.

Except for these tiny crabs, the beach was ominously clean. There was not a single coco-palm frond or other debris from the hurricane. The tidal wave that had buried the three humans had piled an unimaginable amount of pristine offshore sand on the beach, to a depth of over six feet, half a mile or more wide, and a quarter of a mile from the water line inshore. This soggy slurry of quicksand now lay flat and immobile as cement, with barely a dent or wave. The sea shone light blue, eerily like the eyes of the woman three yards away from the man's head.

Now the man could see the water's edge with absolute clarity, important to consider owing to the tides. The man knew that it was the summer solstice, a time of high tides, but before the storm arrived, he hadn't been paying attention to the phases of the moon. No moon at all, or just a sliver of new moon, would mean the tides wouldn't bring the water very far up the beach.

Then, too, it relieved him to think that because the Island was so near the Equator, the high tide would never be as full as farther north or south. He recalled with a shudder that, on his only trip to France, he had expected to walk across to Mont Saint Michel to visit the abbey, but out of ignorance had arrived at high tide, when it was surrounded by very deep, dangerously swift currents.

To deflect his mounting fears, he turned his head and contemplated the beauty of the woman.

"Where were you when the wave came?" he asked in a normal conversational tone. The wind had subsided and he knew his low, resonant voice would reach her.

The woman raised her head and opened her eyes. Had she been taking a catnap, to keep up her strength?

"How long do you think it will it take before somebody comes to rescue us?" she asked in an anguished voice.

"A few hours, maximum," the man lied. "This beach isn't far from a marina and I'm sure they'll come looking for wrecks. Many pricey yachts must have broken loose of their moorings in that wind, not to mention that wave coming through the marina entrance. It's all about money," he stressed to impress the woman.

"Just because we're not far from the marina hardly means they'll check out this beach. It may be days before someone spots us," the woman said sharply, offended by the masculine logic that a woman's fears needed to be assuaged, as if she were a stupid child.

"Mommy! Mommy!" cried the boy, who was listening to them.

Both adults looked at the boy in surprise. Until now they hadn't given him a thought.

"Don't worry, son, your mother's out looking for you," the woman said. "Meanwhile, try not to cry because we have to conserve the water in our bodies."

The boy fell silent and inclined his head to sleep. The woman followed his example. The man stared out to sea looking for the ship that would notice them, although he realized how impossible it would be to spot the three of them. From offshore, they must look exactly like coconuts flung on the sand by the wind.

All at once, the busy little crabs, which had re-emerged as soon as the humans stopped talking, sank back into their burrows in the sand as a great Moor crab advanced slowly towards the man. The crustacean came to a halt close to the man's face, and, for the first time in his life, the man became terrified of a crab. He was no pro, but he certainly had had his fun crab-fishing many times as a boy. He would grab the creature by the back, haul it out of its hiding place, and wave it at the women and children, who would all scream in terror at those legs flailing impotently in the air.

This crustacean's reddish-yellow carapace, pinched at the edges like a pie-crust and still wet in places, seemed particularly diabolical to the man: the red and black teeth of its claws seemed to have emerged straight from hell. The animal stared at him through two beady black eyes sunk in the front edge of its carapace.

The man turned his head toward the woman to appeal for help. Her head was inclined, eyes closed. The boy, too, seemed to be dozing. The man felt like a fool because his imploring look was a reflex: woman and child could not do a thing to help him, any more than he could help himself, buried up to his neck in sand.

He stared back at the crab, which now was moving unhurriedly to the left, lifting its eight legs one by one to a certain rhythm, as if dancing. When it got to a point when the man could barely see it out of the corner of his left eye, it moved all the way around to the right, maintaining its stately prancing rhythm. Apparently, it enjoyed striking terror into its victims and savoring their moments of indecision.

The crab's movements reminded the man of a Hindu dance he had seen in a film. It made him think of temple sculptures of Indian gods with multiple legs and arms. Seeing these sculptures for the first time, he had thought about the thunderous sound those multiple legs would make running across a battlefield, and then the searing whoosh of their multiple arms wielding their myriad swords and spears. Indian gods seemed always armed, raring to go to war.

Something caused the crab to stand up on its rear legs and make threatening movements with its claws, the right larger than the left, opening and closing soundlessly to warn all foes how easy it would be to crush them. The crab must have felt emboldened by the man's terror and conviction that the creature would first go for his eyes.

Moved by gut instinct, the man shouted in his deepest, most resonant voice, not caring whether he woke up the woman and the boy:

"Shoo! Shoo! Shoo!"

The animal, clearly annoyed but also intimidated, lowered its legs and turned, scurrying off sideways at top speed towards the sea.

The woman opened her eyes with a start in time to see the crab disappear into the waves that were now gently dying in the sand. The boy woke up crying. The woman said in a calm voice, to soothe him:

"Don't be afraid, son. It was just a crab."

The woman looked at the man and seemed relieved not to be alone with the child, who closed his eyes and went back to sleep.

The woman began to speak in an unexpected way. "If we aren't rescued in time, I want someone to know that I regret the evil I have done to others. I have never been very religious but I would like to confess," the woman said, as if ashamed.

"Ma'am, I don't believe in God and I am as far from a priest as a person can get. But if it makes you feel better, go ahead and tell me what's weighing on your conscience. I will listen to you with the utmost respect. I am accustomed to having my clients share their most intimate concerns."

She paused, then said, "For one thing, I cheated on my husband because he bores me to death and only ever pays attention to his business. I have taken several lovers and with the last one, I became pregnant. I had not had sex with my husband for a long time, and when I found out I was pregnant I knew I would have to seduce my husband to make him believe that the child was his. But I couldn't bring myself to do it because I didn't want to have to keep up that lie every day – all the same, I refused to kill the fruit of my joy. So, I made up an excuse to spend some months with my parents until the child was born, then gave the baby up for adoption because its father had no interest in taking care of it. When the baby was born, I never held it, or asked to know its sex, the color of its hair or eyes, nothing that might make me attached to it. My parents have kept the secret. My husband, who only cares about money and his work, is clueless. Meanwhile, I feel so guilty. I carry this guilt like an anvil."

She paused. "And you, what great fault do you have to confess?" the woman asked, relieved at having unloaded her own burden.

"I am no friend of confessions," the man said. "Actually, I abhor them. Especially in the confessional, you never know who's listening. But just so you don't imagine I'll take advantage of your sincerity, let me confess: as a private investigator, when I was starting out, one of my first cases came to me through the friend of a wealthy industrialist who suspected his wife was cheating on him. I followed the woman every afternoon for some time as she went to a hotel to meet a man. Finally, I was able to get a shot of them hugging, and showed it to the husband. He was a cold man and stared at the picture, no emotion at all, and I assumed at worst he'd use the photos to divorce the woman. He paid me well and I was very happy. But as I drove off, something like intuition made me go to the hotel and see what I could find out about the man. I discovered that he had recently arrived from Mexico without money. The woman I had been following had been paying for his room." He paused, discomfited.

"She was this man's sister. What her brother's problem was, I never discovered – a drug mess?

"I raced back to my client's house to tell him he had no cause to institute divorce proceedings. But just as I arrived, the woman comes out on the terrace screaming and waving her arms at me, hysterical, begging me to help her. It is as if she knows me, knows I was following her and must now protect her.

"Her husband reached her first and cut her throat with a knife. I took off, terrified, and that night on TV, the news said the husband had lost his mind."

The woman looked at him with horror. "What a dreadful story! You should have done your job! Why didn't you make sure what was really going on?"

The man smiled sadly. "And you, why didn't you avoid having a child with your lover? Why did you give it up for adoption?"

The woman looked wounded and turned away from the man to stare at the sea.

"I'm not criticizing you. I just want you to realize that these things happen and it's very easy to decide afterwards what should or shouldn't have happened. In your case, your child may end up the chief of police somewhere, or, who knows, a famous opera star."

The woman looked at him again and her voice became more understanding. "After what happened to you, did you ever take another case like that?"

The man sighed, suddenly dejected.

"Yes – just one, another industrialist who thought his wife was cheating on him. As cold and busy as the first, he had become suspicious because his wife had begged off sleeping with him for months. I followed her and saw her enter a man's house. This time I made sure: I photographed the couple through a window with my most powerful telephoto lens, shots of them making love, which I developed myself to avoid any possibility of scandal or blackmail. I reported to the husband – but something stopped me from showing him the photos, probably the memory of that other case. I lied and told the husband that his wife was faithful to him and that this estrangement possibly came from his not paying enough attention to her. The husband smiled and told me in a cold voice entirely lacking in feeling: 'Well then, tonight I don't have to kill her.'

"I never again took another domestic surveillance case," the man said, closing his eyes and inclining his head to avoid the woman's glance. He did not want her to read on his face that the reason she seemed so familiar was that it was she whom he had photographed using a telephoto lens in bed with her lover.

The day dragged on. The man looked up. Gauging by the Sun's position, it was around three o'clock in the afternoon, the hottest hour. His face, the back of his neck, his ears – even his hair – felt grilled. His lips were sausages. If he could survive the next couple of hours, the freshness of the sunset breeze and the shadow of night would alleviate things greatly, but for now his head felt par-boiled. The Sun's rays were piling hot stones atop his brains, but there was no point in complaining because the woman and the boy hadn't said a thing for hours. Conceivably, they had fainted in the heat. The man imagined his legs and lower torso suffering from hypothermia down there in the wet, packed sand where the heat of the Sun couldn't reach. From time to time he felt tremors. His lips, beginning to crack, stung when he tried to moisten them with saliva. Breathing was becoming difficult, at times painful: was the sand compacting itself ever more tightly? When he swallowed, he heard ominous gurgles. He was losing his sense of time. What day was it? How many hours they had been buried in the sand? – Had it been days? He worried that maybe he had been passing out on and off, and had lost all track of time.

In the distance, the sea shone like a blue diamond. This would have filled his heart with joy, had he not been in the most desperate situation of his life, unmatched even by the one war he had been sent to as a reservist.

He was startled to see his father, walking on water towards him.

"Be calm, son. It's going to be all right," his father said, looking exactly as he had the day he died, a tall, strong, young man, silhouetted against the blue sky, his loose white dress shirt flapping in the breeze. They smiled at each other with deep affection.

A tinkling of tiny bells and the coolness of sea water around his neck woke the man from a profound sleep. The full moon lit everything with a diamond glow. The little bells were white, brown, and pink stones bumping into each other as they rolled along on the sand under water, herded by gentle waves that came and went, sporadically reaching up to tickle the man's chin. He had been dreaming about slaking his thirst from a spring bubbling up through rocks hemmed in by ferns and moss. The delicious cold of the water flowing down his throat mutated, as he grew more alert, into thirst-producing fire.

He looked around, having no idea where he was until he spotted the heads of the woman and the child, still sticking out of the sand, being lapped at by the same waves. But because the two of them were on a slightly higher mound of sand, the water wasn't lapping at their chins yet. Both seemed to be asleep. He sighed with relief. He could not bear to watch them drown in this shallow rush of seawater.

When the occasional aggressive wave came, the man threw his head back to cool his brains and avoid drowning. This went on all through the night's high tide: the wave would come, he'd look up at the sky, and the white and luminous moon would be sheltering some strange secret that he, the detective, did not want to discover.

By dawn, the cooling sea had retreated and the Sun was back, determined to radiate its heat, hanging there in its cruel, cloudless sky. The woman and the child continued with heads down and eyes closed. Were they in a coma?

"Wake up! Wake UP!" he yelled at them. The woman jerked her head up and looked at him, frightened. The boy continued as he was. "Nothing's happening, I just wanted to know if you were in a coma. The boy may be," said the man, noticing that the child's skin had taken on a blue pallor, perhaps from lack of circulation.

The woman looked at the boy and began to pray.

"Do not pray! For God's sake, save your energy! It would be better for you to go back to sleep and not tire yourself." And yet the woman went on praying. The man shook his head, thinking, Women are so irrational – what good are prayers now? The man had no time for superstitions and was not going to weaken now, when he was possibly close to death.

After a while the woman left off praying and the man regretted it because he enjoyed hearing her voice. Maybe she had a sore throat, or, like him, her mucous membranes were beginning to bleed: he could taste a metallic flavor mixed with his saliva, so thick that it had become more difficult than phlegm to swallow.

He wanted to shout at the gorgeous blue sea, accuse it of indifference, but he had lost the strength to scream. Beginning to intuit death, his limbs were shaking with shorter periodic tremors, and his thoughts were becoming confused. Fragments of memories from his childhood, of his parents, filled his mind. Sometimes he would repeat, out loud, whole conversations his memory was serving up, or just engage in his part of a long-forgotten argument. The sky was cloudless. There was no possibility that rain would fall. When he tried not to think about water, the response his mind gave him was the sensation of fresh, cold liquid assuaging his burning throat, the sound of the childish gulping noise he would make when swallowing, and the bizarre notion that it all sounded like the most beautiful music.

He gazed at the sea to stop thinking about his throat, and saw golden dolphins jumping, tritons riding the waves and blowing on their conch shells. With cheeks inflated like balloons, titanic Boreas – the north wind – and sweet Zephyrus – the west wind – and all those other winds whose names he had forgotten blew their braying horns as they witnessed the birth of Venus, surfing on her giant scallop shell. The sirens produced foam in the sea flapping their silver-scaled tails, singing a wonderful song that would have made the man throw himself into the sea to find these extraordinary creatures. Alas, he thought, if only I were not buried in sand.

The man turned his head to see if the woman wanted to make a comment on this invisible marine pageant, but she was asleep or unconscious.

Or something. Behind the woman's head, he saw a horrendous black wraith hovering in thin air for an instant, then rapidly moving toward them. The black specter closed in, and the man opened his mouth to scream, but no sound emerged.

Disfigured by distance and the mirage effect of hot air rising from the sand, the wraith turned out to be a large, black, exceedingly friendly dog. When it got to the man's head, it treated him like a salt lick, covering every inch of his face with its fragrant tongue. The dog's owner knelt and started digging with his hands. Dutifully, the dog gave up its delighted licking and energetically began to dig too. Soon a crowd was helping disinter the three of them.

"Please, get the boy and the woman out first. I can wait," the man begged, in a choked voice. By the time the man was released from his sand prison, disaster-relief workers had carried off the woman and the boy, intravenous solution dripping into their depleted veins.

Months later, the man and the woman nearly collided in the city's commercial center. She was holding the boy's hand. "The Wave," by now part of the city's mythology, had taken the boy's parents, whose bodies had been found, along with dozens of other missing persons, buried under tons of sand within feet of the "Miracle of the Trinity," the epithet the town had given to the detective, the woman, and the boy.

The woman's husband had been transformed because, he said, God's grace had safeguarded the life of his spouse. He had beseeched her on his knees, in view of many townspeople, to renew their vows of matrimony – and even asked her to consider taking in the boy.

Seeing the woman there in the commercial center, the man, who had given up detective work to become a teacher, smiled with delight.

"Ma'am, I'm overjoyed to run into you! What happiness it gives me to see the boy!" he exclaimed.

"Oh no! No! Please no!" the woman cried, dragging the boy away at a run. What would it avail her to reminisce with this person who had shared her hours of greatest despair, those terrible moments when she thought she was going to die? Determined to erase from her mind the wave that had buried her, and all that had gone before, she would not learn that the wave that had reunited her with her husband had also restored to its birth mother the baby she had given up for adoption. Finding out everything he could about the boy and his drowned parents had been the former detective's last investigation, which he had undertaken when it occurred to him to adopt the boy himself.

HOMECOMING

I walk down a spotless street in my neighborhood, heading home at noon, the raging heat of the intense white Antillean Sun pounding my head like a hammer. I'm in the middle of the street because there are no cars coming from either direction and, as far as I can see, the street is completely deserted. I'm surprised not to hear birds chirping or see them flying around. The silence is total, except for the spectral sound of my footsteps bouncing off the walls of the houses.

As I climb the stairs to my house, I'm surprised to find the front door wide open. Inside, I hear a monotonous noise, like a flapping of wings. In the dining room, on the table covered by a red-and-white checkered cloth, the breeze from a small fan's blades agitates three yellow ribbons tied to its safety mesh. In my room, a cool wind redolent of ocean and trees lifts the transparent white chiffon curtains. The dark green walls impart the heat of the Sun in fumes smelling of jasmine and tasting like mint. Exhausted by the long journey, I stretch out on my bed's woven white spread. The snail-like expansion-and-contraction of the curtains in the breeze reminds me of nights in my teens when I would lie there and the full moon would pour its milky light on me while the chiffon rose and fell and the warm, vibrant scent of gardenias wafted in. Now, the burden of years weighs down my eyelids.

I open my eyes and it's no longer noon, but I have no idea how long I've slept. The afternoon has made its peace with the Sun, its gentle rays now awakening faint orange reflections on the wall. I get up and head to the kitchen for a glass of water. A small crocodile-shaped magnet is holding up a note on the refrigerator door: "We're waiting for you over at Alta's! Manolo asked us to help out with dinner." I march over to my aunt Alta's house, only a few blocks away, and find my uncle Manolo hanging a string of colored lights on the porch.

"Look who's here!" he shouts, and my relatives pour out the front door, cheering and clapping. "How tall she is! She looks like an American!" says Alta, giving me a hug that buries me inside her huge wine-red velvet house pajamas.

I'm followed into the living room by everyone. My aunt Cacha is perched on a wooden stepladder trying to fasten a silver angel on top of a huge Christmas tree covered in green, blue, red, gold, silver balls, lit by colorful candle-shaped lights with bubbles dancing in brightly colored liquid.

"Aren't you *not* supposed to celebrate Christmas?"

My relatives look at each other and laugh.

"See what happens when you spend too much time abroad?" Manolo points out to everybody, as if to apologize for my ignorance.

The fluffy cotton meant to look like snow under the tree is piled with gift boxes, wrapped in handsome colored papers secured with fancy ribbons. "Where on earth did you get these gifts? There's nothing in the stores here!" I say, unable to suppress my astonishment.

"No, no, no, no," Manolo replies, smiling, and takes me by the arm over to the Nativity on one side of the tree. "Look at the Nativity we put together this year! The pieces are all Italian!" Manolo informs me.

Inside the manger, lit from behind by a heavenly blue light shaped like a star, the figures of the Virgin Mary, Joseph, three kneeling shepherds, and an angel gather behind the cradle where a baby Jesus rests. All these figures were made by "a real artist," Manolo avers. Plodding through the cotton snow, three camels transport the Wise Men, Gaspar, Balthasar and Melchior, their luxurious garments painted in beautiful, intense colors edged with gold leaf. I can't imagine how my family has managed to procure these things. I've seen pictures of people in the city, including professionals, rifling through trash because they don't earn enough to eat. Very few people, just those who have access to foreign currencies and state officials, are able to go with euros to the tourist shops, the only ones that offer any real merchandise.

Cacha finishes positioning the finial with the angel to her satisfaction, and descends from the heights of the wooden stepladder.

"Let me see you up close!" she exclaims, inspecting me as if in doubt that I am the same person. "You're not young, but you've aged well. How was your flight? Did you have any problems?" she asks as if fishing for a compliment.

"Not at all. Everything went perfectly."

It's as if they don't know what to do and I don't know what to say until two kids run into the room. An eight-year-old girl, very like my cousin Silvia, is chasing a seven-year-old boy, very like my cousin Luisito.

"Fairy! Faggot! Thief!" the girl shouts.

"Damn it! You devils!" exclaims Cacha, running after them to give them a smack, all three disappearing down the hall leading to the interior of the house.

"Who are these kids?" I ask Manolo.

"They're Cacha's – they're your cousins Silvia and Luisito! Don't you remember them? But let's everybody sit down. We're all hovering around you like you're a freak." I sit in a great padded armchair in the living room. My relatives distribute themselves attentively in the other armchairs and on the brown sofa embroidered with golden thread.

"It can't be! When I left, they were teenagers," I say, shaking my head in astonishment.

Everyone laughs and looks at each other again. Now I can see my uncles and aunts haven't aged either. "You're just in time for the feast to begin. Fili is finishing roasting the piglet in the yard," says Uncle Luis, smiling as he comes down the hall.

"My father?" I ask, horrified.

"Is there another Fili in this family?" Luis replies, as if I were an idiot. He leads me by the hand out to the backyard, a grassy slope descending to a sidewalk. My father is turning a spit with a piglet impaled on it over a fire's leaping flames. I know perfectly well that my father is dead, but I am not going to express surprise. I don't trust these people and I'm determined to be cautious until I understand what this is all about.

"You're just in time to taste the hot piglet," my father tells me with a smile.

"Make it really well done. I love crispy skin," I reply, letting go of Luis' hand. My father laughs and points with his index finger at my mother, who's sitting on a wooden folding chair a way off on the lawn.

"Go say hi to the old lady – she's been really worried about you," he says jovially.

I pull up another folding chair in front of my mother. She's dead too, I know, but I smile at her in greeting.

"You look great," I say sincerely, because she is very well dressed and made up.

My mother smiles and tells me she's ecstatic that I've returned, but her eyes express great suffering.

"What's the matter? What are you worried about?" I ask her quietly in case she's afraid my father and Luis are listening. My mother casts a terrified glance over my head. I turn around to look. Four military Jeeps bump up onto the sidewalk at the foot of the lawn. Soldiers armed with automatic rifles array themselves in a semi-circle on the lawn, blocking any escape.

My relatives file out into the yard with sad faces. My father stops roasting the piglet, joining Luis and the others. All put on long faces. My mother gets up from her chair and walks over to stand with everyone. They all look like actors at the final curtain of some dour theatrical performance.

A senior officer overtakes the soldiers and moves towards me. The enormous machine gun in his hand is pointing to the ground. As he approaches, I recognize my brother. "It took a while to convince you to come. But at last you're here!" He laughs, raises the machine gun and pushes the tip of the barrel against my heart.

My eyes pop open. The flight attendant has bumped me with her elbow as she removed the food tray in front of my seat.

"I'm so sorry," she apologizes.

The captain's clear voice is heard over the loudspeaker: "Ladies and gentlemen, if you look down, those of you sitting on the left side of the cabin will see that we are now flying over Cuba. We will shortly be commencing our descent to Miami International Airport." I'm on the left side, in a window seat in business class on this long flight returning from a South American country, where I interviewed that country's vice president and many business owners on the state of one of their booming industries.

The clouds clear, and a vast green expanse becomes visible below. Several large, long grey buildings sit side by side, like prison barracks. I feel an electric current going through my spine. I am terrified to think that this aircraft might crash right there, on that field, and I might survive the crash.

NEW EXPERIENCES

The enormous muscular black man pulls a gun from his belt and shoves it into the white kid's mouth.

"You want me to blow your brains out, white boy?"

"White boy" goes liver-colored. The kid has dreamed of living a moment like this, with the scene in slow motion because life is supposedly marching you through your memories, letting you ponder, before you die, all the idiotic things you've ever done. Now the moment has come and it's clear there won't be time for pondering anything.

"Easy now, brother, I spoke in ignorance. I'm not from this neighborhood," the kid replies, trying to keep his voice from changing octaves, not to sound like an idiotic Upper East Side sissy. With the cold, bitter-tasting barrel in his mouth, what he says comes out "Eevy nah, brah, ah fpoakh nuh ignranf! Nah fum bif daibrrhb!"

The black man smiles. Fear: you can smell it a mile off. He turns his head and, pointing to the kid with a gesture of his mouth, asks the light-skinned girl sitting on the other side of him, "Honey, this your bro?"

Reflected in the bar's long mirror, behind the liquor bottles, the light-skinned girl leans forward, looks the white youth up and down, and says snippily: "My brother? Nossiree, that is not my brother. My brother is on 125th Street, watching telly-vision."

Grateful that the girl's wit makes the regulars at the bar laugh, mostly blacks and Latinos, the kid tentatively smiles and the tension dissolves. The black man removes the gun from the kid's mouth, dries the saliva off it with the paper napkin from under his scotch on the rocks, and tucks the weapon into his belt in the middle of his back, covering it with his leather jacket. He smiles at the white kid with the whitest, evenest teeth the kid has ever seen. The kid coughs to disguise his trembling and takes a sip from his martini with a lemon peel.

"What brings you here?" the black man asks, as if he hadn't just been tickling the kid's tonsils with a gun.

"I'm looking for new experiences. This is the neighborhood of artists. I apologize if I offended you earlier by saying that painting of a mermaid looks like her," the kid explains, pointing to the light-skinned girl and looking again at the large oil painting on the wall above the mirror, a naked woman with a resplendent silver tail.

"She's Miss Miller to you, White Boy. Miss Mia Miller," he growls.

"Leroy, give it a rest! In fact, that is me," the girl says, looking directly at the kid.

"It's a very nice painting, Miss Miller," the kid says softly.

Mia smiles. "Call me Mia," she says. "What's your name?"

"I'm Bob. It's nice to meet you, Mia."

Bob and Mia smile at each other in the mirror. The black man frowns and takes a sip of his drink. "Well, my name's Leroy and it's time for me to go. Mia, you want something, you know where to find me."

Leroy slides his butt off the bar stool and turns to leave without giving Bob another glance. Bob looks up and down at Leroy, calculating his height to be about seven feet. At five-eight, Bob feels like a child.

"Is Leroy your boyfriend?"

"Nah, we're just friends. Friends since we were little. He's very protective. Sometimes we hang out here at the bar. Leroy has a white chick, but he won't go out with her because she's very jealous and doesn't give him space."

Bob is captivated by Mia's golden skin and green eyes, but all he can talk about is Leroy.

"So, is Leroy a police officer?" Bob asks. "I noticed his weapon is a Glock, like the NYPD uses."

"No, he just has some police friends and sometimes guns, you know, go missing in the precincts. Leroy 'found' one. You police?"

"I just watch TV shows about cops and detectives."

Mia pulls a puppet of the comic-strip dog Pluto out of her purse and sets it on the counter next to her beer. Pluto's butt connects by a long flexible blue tube to a small blue rubber ball, like the ones that come with perfume atomizers. Mia smiles at Bob and squeezes the blue ball, making the dog adopt pornographic poses.

Bob watches intently.

"I know a hotel nearby where we can spend some time together," says Mia softly, while Pluto runs through his repertory.

Mia stamps her brown leather boots on the linoleum floor of the hotel's fire-engine-red hall, and the sound reverberates with a bleak echo. Between every two doors, there's a low-watt yellow bulb hanging from the ceiling. Mia stops at a door, looks at Bob with a wicked smile and turns the key in the lock. The room is dim. A bit of light from street lamps filters through the window's dirty glass, sloppily brushed with green paint on the inside, eliminating the need for curtains but letting in a few bleak rays.

Mia tosses the key onto a plastic table and drops her rabbit-fur coat on a seedy chair. Bob shrugs off his suede jacket and hangs it on the bedstead. Mia extends her open hand. Bob smiles, pulls out his ostrich leather wallet, slips out a twenty, and puts it in her hand. Mia keeps her hand outstretched. Bob pulls out another couple of bills.

"I don't carry credit cards. This is all the money I have left after paying for the drinks and the room," Bob says apologetically, smiling to hide his embarrassment.

A shape emerges from the gloom and moves toward Mia and Bob. Of course it's Leroy – who could mistake that gigantic form?

"You shittin' me – fifty, that's all?" Leroy says.

"Nobody comes down here with so little money!" Mia says, concern in her voice.

"Nobody!" Leroy echoes. "Did you think you'd get robbed? You are going to take us home with you and pay us fair wages." Leroy says this as if he were a union rep talking to a company manager.

Bob puts his jacket back on and leaves the room followed by Leroy and Mia. He has no idea what these two are up to, but he knows all about Leroy's Glock, not to mention his being strong as an Olympic wrestler and seven feet tall. There's no way he can defend himself. It's going to be whatever Leroy says, unless he can come up with a plan.

Sitting between Mia and Leroy in a cab, Bob is dismayed as the cabbie angles over to Park, making great time through a New York resplendent with Christmas decorations in this late afternoon. The city seems different to Bob. He notices the buildings in great detail; it strikes him that his eyes have never seen so clearly. He marvels at the magical columns of blue smoke that rise up in the middle of the street from the underworld of Manhattan, this city that he has seen all his protected life without paying much attention. Women look more beautiful and elegant striding purposefully up the broad sidewalks of Park, barely casting a glance at the occasional boutique or gallery.

When the cabbie finally cuts over to head down Fifth Avenue and pull up at his building, Bob is relieved and pleased that the doorman respectfully calls him Mr. Bell and runs to press the elevator button, without even a sideways glance at Mia and Leroy, who don't look very different from Bob's usual friends, his fellow students at Columbia. So relieved that his parents are in London for the week, Bob sighs when the elevator door opens on the foyer of his parents' apartment, his safe space. He opens the front door with his key and, as if she has been here before, Mia plunges past him into the living room with its panoramic glass wall. She slides the balcony door open and stretches out her arms to embrace what's left of the yellow and purple sky in the West.

"Now, this is the life!" Mia shouts with joy, turning her head to look at Bob, who slips his house key into his pants pocket and drops his jacket on the glass table in the dining room. Leroy, following Bob's lead, throws his leather jacket on the table, covering Bob's.

"I've dreamed my whole life of seeing Central Park from the top of a Fifth Avenue building," Mia sighs from the balcony, calmly enjoying the glow from the setting Sun and the mostly lit windows of Central Park West, the opposite side of those hundreds of acres of bare trees, dry grass and disintegrating patches of sooty snow that will fill in with lush grass months from now.

"First, let's have you pay us back the money we loaned you for the cab," Leroy says. "If I'd known it was so expensive, we could have taken the subway." Leroy is taking the tone of an avuncular businessman warning his son not to be so profligate in the future.

Bob lifts a Picasso off its hanger, opens the wall safe, takes out a small tube of hundred-dollar bills tightly rolled in the shape of a cigarette, and hands it to Leroy.

"You really are a spoiled honkey brat! Who hands over bills like that without counting every single one?" Mia scolds Bob in alarm as she comes in from the balcony, taking off her coat and tossing it onto a leather sofa.

Leroy separates the bills and sniffs them, dropping them disdainfully, one by one, onto the dining table's glass surface, where they bounce and all individually curl up, almost alive.

"They all covered in cocaine, like every other dollar in the world. They's a grand here," he says triumphantly. Ten little green tubes, determined not to give up their utilitarian shape.

"A small fortune," says Mia pointedly.

"Not so. When you consider the inflation we're going to have," Leroy corrects, "this is – how you say – inadequate." He walks over to the safe, which Bob has neglected to close, and lifts out several thick banded bundles of hundred-dollar bills and tosses them onto the glass table top. The ten hundred-dollar tubes do a little dance of greeting.

"My god," Mia says. "Who keeps cash like this in their house?"

"I calculate we got half a million bucks here." Code-switching to the diction of a Wall Street investment counselor on TV, Leroy says, "Invested conservatively, say at four percent, that'll give us a retirement income of twenty thousand dollars a year, right? As they say, it's a start. You know, a kind of economic firewall," Leroy says.

Bob is sulking. "You've emptied the safe and haven't given me a thing in return," he whines, slouching at the table with a sad look in his honey-colored eyes. A lock of blond, straight hair falls across his white forehead, casting a slight shadow over his transparent skin and rosy cheeks. Bob looks like he realizes he's missed something – his chance to escape, while Leroy was rooting around in the safe, or maybe he's rebuking himself for not being able to act, after telling himself he would just wait for the right moment.

But his heart is somewhere else.

From behind, Leroy lifts him by the armpits right out of his chair and drags him to the balcony. With a single quick gesture, Leroy has him by the ankles, gives him a taste of what it's like to be hanging upside-down, then swings him over the railing with all the grace of a shot-putter, bumping him against the edge of the balcony. Bob has the presence of mind to cross his arms, protecting his face. Leroy has an iron grip on his ankles, and upside-down, Bob is able to see inside the darkened living room of the apartment below. Nobody's home yet. Bob feels his face turn red and his ears buzz. Stretching his neck back lets him see straight down twenty stories, Fifth Avenue lit by headlights and streetlamps and marquees with doormen waiting to hold doors open for owners returning home to tasty dinners with fine Bordeaux. Bob, beginning to be nauseated, can hear the cars and buses stop and go and honk at each other impatiently when the light changes. He can see shoulders of some pedestrians, but not once do any of these fine boulevardiers turn and look up. He could scream to the passers-by, but Leroy would let him drop.

"Do you think to accuse us of stealing, bitch?" Leroy says with ancestral rage. Adrenaline has filled his muscles with superhuman strength and he jerks Bob up a foot, lets him hang in thin air, then grabs him by the calves, and squeezes as if he wants to crush Bob's tibias and fibulas and blood vessels.

"Leroy, you crazy? You stop hurting that boy!" Mia shouts, pounding his back with her fists.

Leroy breathes deeply and pulls himself together. He yanks Bob back from the urban cliff keeping his iron grip on his chubby calves, then dropping him on the balcony tiles like a doll.

Drawing his knees up to his chest and rubbing his bruised calves, Bob takes big deep breaths before defending himself. "I never accused anybody of anything. I never once meant to offend you."

Leroy stares at him. "On your feet, boy. We going inside." Leroy pulls the sliding glass door shut and marches Bob back to one of the bedrooms, which he figures is Bob's owing to its framed posters of old movies and photos of James Dean and model airplanes hanging on black threads from the ceiling. Mia follows.

Leroy stares at Bob and tells Mia to gag him with a handkerchief or a necktie, undress him, and tie his limbs to the four posts using the hundreds of neckties and belts hanging in the large walk-in closet, the door to which Bob left open when he got dressed for his little outing and whose extensive contents are illuminated with funky neon lights.

Mute and immobile, Bob watches Mia follow Leroy's instructions. Clearly, he wishes that what is happening would end, and that tomorrow, when he wakes up, it will all turn out to have been just a nightmare. The only reason he went to that bar was to feel free at least briefly while his parents were away. He regrets not being able to count on them materializing to coddle him as they have all his life, his mother to surprise him with strawberry tartlets from Fortnum & Mason, a decorative bottle of orange liqueur.

Not a chance they will arrive tonight. The housekeeper will come in the morning, let herself in with her key, and all hell will break loose.

"What you were going to do, do it now," Leroy orders Mia.

"Well, hallelujah, brother, sometimes you just go too far to get me excited..." Mia removes her clothing making lustful movements like a stripper, while Leroy pokes around Bob's bookshelf full of pornography.

"Well, well, well," Leroy says, gleefully snatching a first edition of erotic poems by ee cummings off a bookshelf and flipping through it, as if he is looking for one specific poem.

Bob is furious because, like a little boy, he can't control his erection as he watches Mia's seductive dance. Sex is a shameful thing, and he would rip out this stupid penis of his at this moment, if his hands weren't tied.

"I'm amazed this boy has something so...*ag-gres-sive,*" says Leroy pointing his finger at the young man and admiring his rosy flesh, his luscious body, so well fed and cared for.

Mia slips a condom on the center of attention and sits on it, rising and falling gently as if riding a horse.

Leroy reads the ee cummings poem he was looking for with a deep, passionate voice:

> *i like to feel the thorn*
> *of your body and your bones, and the shuddering*
> *— firm — softness that i*
> *again and again and again*
> *kiss, I like to kiss your this and your that,*
> *i like slowly caressing the shocking hair*
> *of your electric fur, and what's-it coming*
> *on your parted flesh...*

Mia bursts into laughter at the poem as she comes and Bob ejaculates at the same time. Bob has never had such an orgasm. His entire body vibrates.

Leroy puts the book back on its shelf, sets the gun on the nightstand, and strips quickly, tossing his faded jeans and blue worker's shirt, so popular among writers and artists, on the floor. Naked, Leroy walks around the bed, studying Bob closely, letting Bob get a good look at his long, thick, inflamed sex. He shows off his sexual pride, likes how his muscular body looks in the walk-in closet mirror, enjoys displaying his power, particularly there in Bob's room.

"Time to go, Leroy. Let him be." Mia says curtly, tossing him his clothes while she dresses herself. "Take a cold shower or something, but let's get a move on."

Leroy thinks about it, then puts on his clothes slowly and deliberately with his eye on Bob, as if to say, "You have no idea what I'm capable of." Then he shoves the Glock in his belt with a tomorrow's-another-day gesture, and follows Mia out of the room.

After a few minutes, Bob hears them slam the apartment door and feels immense relief at being alone. He dozes off cooking up what he'll tell the housekeeper the next morning when she finds him tied up naked on the bed with a condom drooping off his deflated penis.

FIFTH COLUMN

I come from the war and I'll be back at it in a few days. My father's dying and I hope that I, his only son, arrive in time to hear his last gasp. He's a general, military through and through, as am I, his only son, and that gasp – because he's dying in bed and not on the battlefield – will be the snarl of the warlord, like the rabid roar of Alexander when he had to return to Babylon and renounce the conquest of India.

I'm on a commercial flight, by special dispensation that some of my fellow officers envied without knowing that I envy them. I don't like leaving the war because it's been my life's purpose. I've been trained to kill, like all my ancestors. If I were Japanese, I'd belong to a samurai family. Though I'm not Japanese but American, I admire Bushido, the code of conduct adhered to by the samurai, those gods of war whose nobility most soldiers today can't match. My ancestors in the Middle Ages, who earned fame and fortune in England with their brave swords, would have followed Bushido.

What I despise about war today is its cowardice. Men fight by pressing buttons and triggers, using grenade launchers like machine guns, carpet bombing from drones. My ancestors fought the enemy man to man, inflicted and received wounds, inhaled the sour, boar-like scent of the enemy.

I know Alexander would have used modern weapons without hesitation, and I too use them, but I prefer to kill the enemy with my bare hands, expose my chest to my enemy's knife. This is how you savor the rapture of battle and the triumph of survival. That's the way to develop courage, to get rid of your weak knees and your fluttering heart, to advance on the path to Glory.

The appetizing smell of food heating up in the plane's galley brings to mind, in contrast, the pungent stench of Kuwait's burnt-out wells, those nights that lasted longer than the Bible's famous three days, lit up only by the glare of those columns of fire with their orange and red edges. Some of those flares rose to the sky in the shape of angels with open wings, exhaling plumes of black smoke toward the horizon.

It was in the first Gulf War that I got my captain's bars and medals for bravery in action, for inspiring the platoon I commanded as first lieutenant. In that battle of lies we were chasing an invisible enemy that abandoned it all – battle tanks, AFVs, artillery – in the sand and, on top of that, set fire to oil wells as they fled. It was during that action that my men started calling me Ares, god of war. A student of Greek mythology who enlisted to pay for college gave me the nickname. I played along with the joke and asked my father to see if he could find a wearable replica of an ancient Greek helmet, and I'll be damned if he didn't! So every time we went into action, I'd wear it to cheer the boys up.

Then, in Iraq, I'd stand in the turret of a tank or behind the gun in an AFV, wearing my Ares helmet. I kept that red plume waving in the wind every time we went on some nasty mission, and my group became the most effective in the coalition. Now, without fail, every time my group returns from a mission, they say with heroic mockery when asked about their experience: "The horror! The horror!"

My flight lands in Atlanta without any turbulence, right on time. I'm waved through customs and a female driver in uniform holding up a sign with my name on it is waiting at the exit. "Captain Andrew Brooke?" the driver asks me as I approach. I nod my head, and she opens the door to a black Mercedes.

I duck inside, unbutton my dress coat, and ease back into the cushy seat. I'm exhausted from the trip and woozy from the drinks I had on the plane, imagining my father dying or dead. But I'm still awake enough to be surprised that the old man sent me a uniformed driver in a Mercedes, when he hates those uniforms (let alone women in uniform) and had a BMW. Well, maybe he's changed his taste in cars – mellowed – and hired a driver while I've been in country.

We're speeding up I75 to connect with Georgia 400, and I lower the tinted window to refresh my eyes and nose with the fragrance of pines, the green elms all leafed-out, the tall ash trees draped in wisteria and lavender on both sides of the road. We take the Peachtree exit, and I'm dazzled by the lemon-yellow bells of the daffodils, the red geraniums, the white and yellow daisies, the azaleas blanketed in red, orange, white, purple and yellow flowers. How exhausting is that desiccated terrain, those dust storms that infiltrate every fold of your skin right down to your navel – what a change, this endless vegetation, this verdant fertility! Now, if only Atlanta could get rid of those clouds of golden pollen swirling through the streets, to purify that cool spring wind! I'll be very glad to see the Ionic columns of our family home in Roswell, saved from the Atlanta fire ordered by General Sherman in the War Between the States.

The driver turns hard right. "Miss, this is not the way!" I snap.

"I'm stopping at my house for just a sec, Captain. We're just a few minutes away," the driver apologizes, looking back and smirking deferentially. I'm surprised at the cheekiness of this girl, but it's just not worth it to protest.

The driver pulls into the garage of a house painted green, gets out without saying a word, knocks on the door, and goes inside. Two men dressed in black pop out. One opens the car door and gestures for me to exit the vehicle. Which I do, to my surprise. Then I sense the taller of the two men behind me, poking what feels like a gun into my right kidney.

"There must be some mistake," I say, the last platitude I ever expected to hear myself say. Oh, how I regret not wearing my Beretta – how stupid that sidearms are not allowed on commercial flights.

The men push me inside the house and down a stairwell leading to a windowless basement with dingy walls that smell of mold.

Both the driver and the two men look like Americans, not Arabs. The driver doesn't speak with an accent. I'm in America, not Iraq. This can't happen here. But it *is*. I remember the advice given to me by Colonel Miller, my first commanding officer. "Never let your guard down. Not ever." Now I'm caught like a rat because I believe the U.S. is friendly territory.

One of the men gives me a pamphlet accusing our country of genocide and tells me to memorize it – again, he has no accent – to repeat it into a video camera they've set up on a tripod in front of me.

"I refuse to do any such thing," I say forcefully, reciting my name, rank, and serial number. In a heartbeat, the two men strip me naked, secure my feet and hands, and connect electrodes to my most sensitive parts. I endure the first electric shock, but the second, more powerful and longer, makes me scream for them to stop. In a matter of seconds, I've become willing to say and do whatever they want to keep from feeling that unendurable pain again. I, so brave in the face of death on the battlefield, am a craven coward, like that old cowboy song, when another human being sets out deliberately to make me feel excruciating pain. How could I have known? Yes, "the soldier's life is suffering and sacrifice," according to Colonel Miller, but we don't all have the same physical tolerance, or at least this is what I say to myself.

They dress me again, push me to memorize the pamphlet, quiz me, make me repeat the entire pile of horse manure straight through until I can do it flawlessly. They are patient but adamant, assisted by the menace of electrodes. Finally, to my surprise I find I know the entire text like a role for the theatre. They duct-tape my legs to the chair and turn on the camera. The two men and the woman stand behind me wearing black hoods. I stare at the red light and vomit up accusations and denunciations against the US government and the US Army, my pride and joy, meanwhile praying for my father to die before he sees this dishonorable, shameful video.

What surprises me, however, is that this betrayal hurts me no more than the electric shocks. They'll understand, I tell myself.

Everyone will know that I have been tortured into making this statement.

When I'm done talking, I'm perplexed that they don't turn the camera off, but I feel relief looking at the little red light.

That's until some fingers yank my forehead back, and the edge of a knife slides down the skin of my neck under my Adam's apple, then quickly cuts through skin and cartilage. I let out a sharp, desperate howl, an animal shriek like a stabbed wild boar. The men shout words so loud that I can't hear my own cries of agony. A whistling noise accompanies the air bubbling out of my trachea, followed by a sucking sound as my lungs uncontrollably imbibe blood.

ODYSSEY OF THE THING

I

After a lightning encounter with a philosopher of Logical Positivism, a preacher of the doctrines of Swami Vivekananda, and a guru of Vedanta and Yoga, Mr. Aristides Rivera, a steel-and-oil magnate of indeterminate Latin origin, retired to his penthouse on the top floor of the five-sided Grand Hotel New Babel in Chicago, Illinois. His gigantic single room had the remarkable shape of a dodecahedron made of glass pentagons, its five-sided base anchored tightly to the crown of the hotel's five-sided tube frame. Above the machinery controlling the air conditioning tanks and compressors, elevators, water towers, and emergency generators sat this technological masterpiece, uniting the extremes of ancient Greek architecture and New World vulgarity. This remarkable schizophrenic structure came to be known as the New Babel Room, for reasons obvious to the few who were invited to visit.

From that environment, Aristides could contemplate panoramic sunsets overlapped by the peaks of portentous high rises, fearsome mountain ranges of office and residential buildings that receded into the distance without giving any sign that the strained last breaths of the industrial revolution were undermining them. In Aristides' New Babel Room, however, everything was exposed, revealed, accessible, obtainable. The panes of glass and solar panels making up the extraordinary glittering ball disguised receivers, transmitters, sensors, lenses that provided Aristides with access to information that all the governments of the world would kill for, were they not so terrified of knowing.

This knowledge had transported Aristides to a new stage in life. He now meditated on the sacred art of not-meditating, dedicated his powers of concentration to not-thinking, and articulated the uselessness of articulating. Having slipped through the narrow door of contradiction and walked across the razor edge of mind-lessness, he'd concluded that his mind had not yet reached its terrifying potential. He'd come to believe that his idle neurons were siphoning nutrients from his blood without providing the slightest benefit to his brain. This opinion was owed to his steel-magnate-style humanistic upbringing – that is, to his mediocre Latin and his contempt for those technological metaphors that are the apotheosis of man.

Aristides focused the lenses of his optical equipment to combine a few romantic images of the sunset into that day's work of art, then turned his attention to an article in *The End of Times*, Opus Dei's magazine. Suddenly he looked up, scratched his chin, and found himself formulating the outlandish project of bringing all his neurons to life simultaneously and permanently.

He would overwhelm his nervous system with infinite data, calculations, theories, equivalencies, and squarings of the circle. Out came his cellphone to speed-dial his "assistant." At once a cloud of technicians, scientists, musicians, and astrologers filled the endless screens of the immense room with the buzz of their conversations. Symposia, congresses, conferences were improvised, supplemented by cable TV, movies, YouTube, Kab-balah, Koran, Freemasons, Rosicrucians, Islamic terrorists, the CIA, the FBI, all the social media, and, of course, rock stars, as well as a few top models standing by to be flown in from Milan.

For months Aristides stuffed himself with knowledge. His voraciousness was infinite, and time was entirely at his disposal. Having allocated all his resources to completely investigating everything that exists, that has once existed, and (with some margin for error) that will come to exist, Aristides recognized that this arduous labor was akin to that indulged in by certain Florentine polymaths of the Italian Renaissance, and he wondered if they, too, had experienced the consequences of lost adipose tissue, weakened muscles, alarming baldness. For his study had made Aristides look like a humanoid from some classic science fiction movie.

II

The disturbing conclusions Aristides was reaching thanks to his newly awakened neurons and (to give credit where it's due) also to Apple's latest intergalactic and post-nuclear inventions, caused him to realize that he must warn humanity of his discovery of terrible danger looming soon.

He had reached the astounding conclusion that, in the very near future, humanity would be *too expensive.* Humans would be consuming three times what they produced, leading the planet to an apocalyptic but unambiguous economic crisis that was already driving the plutocracy to replace humans with robots. This was "divine simplicity" all over again.

Robots, no matter what they cost to develop, were cheaper than humans. Robots didn't need food or anything beyond shelter from moisture, excess heat, and cold – and, of course, electrical outlets and solar panels. They didn't need clothes, let alone a spectacular, ever-renewing wardrobe. They didn't reproduce. They didn't create waste. They saved oxygen. They didn't concoct irritating political theories. The world would be in the hands of a few families well known to us all, admired for their bureaucratic efficiency.

This sinister plan, already afoot and scheduled for execution in the mid-twenty-first century, had become apparent to Aristides when he implemented, in the last stage of his investigation, non-Euclidean geometry applied to the mirror image of pi-meson atoms.

He had taken this shortcut because his brain had become hypertrophied by constant study. As his ingenious work-arounds had led to evolving new systems, laws of probabilities, and innovative conclusions, he devoted himself to finding more efficient ways to disseminate information and warn humanity of the danger facing it, and also reveal how humanity might save itself. Of course, he had done some PowerPoint lectures at TED Talks, but a new method of delivery became essential because often, at the end of his talks, people in the audience would become agitated and belligerent, unfairly turning their wrath on Aristides.

The same incendiary information went unremarked when he tried to deliver it individually to subscribers on their cellphones. Now he was competing with cable TV summaries, podcasts of people's personal problems, Facebook, Twitter, not to mention the newest uninfected forms of mass communication, complete with horoscopes. His alarming real evidence was just one more annoyance in this swollen electronic stream.

It was frustrating enough that the human ostriches sticking their heads in the sand refused to give thought to Aristides' findings. But eventually the reaction to Aristides' work came to be divided between ostriches and hostiles, and the ostriches began to repeat the sobriquets hostiles had formulated for Aristides: "Vociferous Hydrocephalus" was used in traditional English-language print media, "The Humanoid" when they needed to save space.

At the same time, the Hispanic media in New York, Miami, Chicago, Los Angeles, and El Paso, great lovers of nicknames, won the brevity sweepstakes by referring to Aristides as "La Cosa" (The Thing). And, of course, *El Miami Herald* couldn't resist calling La Cosa's admonitions "Trotskyite." It wasn't long before the Anglo media adopted "The Thing," without appending antiquated pejorative political characterizations.

One afternoon, Aristides was giving a TED Talk on the relationship between Marduk's fifty names, Disneyworld, and the array of cyclotrons at the Illinois Institute of Technology, which was only a few blocks away from the University of Chicago auditorium where he was speaking. Happily connecting these disparate phenomena to world population growth, he was unaware that all the image orthicons inside the TV cameras melted as they captured the glamorous image of Miss Universe as she walked into that august Chicago auditorium.

Ending his speech with a slogan cribbed from ancient Roman demagogues ("Down with the plutocrats!"), Aristides was amazed to hear a voice coming from Miss Universe interrupt the audience's hulla-baloo with a naïve question: "What makes you so concerned about humanity, when there is absolutely nothing human about you?"

That year's Universal Sex Object had posed a question so reminiscent of naïve but germane queries from stunning blondes of the previous century, such as Marilyn Monroe, that The Thing was left defenseless. The idea that not the slightest progress had been accomplished in human awareness reduced him to babbling hopelessly on the stage, crushed under the horrific weight of ridicule. He who had over-prepared himself to debate with geniuses, scientists, literary critics, and even dialecticians of world history, abjuring all that was bombastic, had neglected to inoculate himself against mindlessness. And in stupidity he had found his Waterloo.

A grand passion arose from that embarrassing instant, transporting The Thing to every ridiculous extreme of unrequited love. But to the flirtatious blonde beauty queen, The Thing could only be a monster of unmatched hideousness. His instantly falling in love with her had made her feel nauseated and chilled.

To escape The Thing's persistent wooing, Miss Universe fled to California to meditate. She joined a Buddhist Kapalika sect in a cave on the Pacific Coast, smeared herself with ashes and surrounded herself with human skulls. The Thing, unaware of all this and unable, despite his vast technological resources, to find her, was reduced to gloomy muteness. He sent misanthropic, macabre letters to newspapers and TV shows, rode an old-folks tricycle with an orange warning flag through the corridors of his hotel, and subscribed to *Reader's Digest*. Eventually he came out as a devil's advocate on talk radio.

After three tedious years and a thousand sighs The Thing decided to reintegrate into the world. Aided by Scientology and Rastafarianism, The Thing commissioned an ocean liner and christened it *Love*, in homage to his catatonic period.

Aristides was reborn on the afternoon he broke a bottle of champagne on *Love*'s hull. It wasn't "Knowledge" that he needed

("He who adds science, adds pain") but rather muscles and dynamic tension. Revived by these thoughts of the flesh, he enrolled in a gym and started lifting weights, and doing boxing, calisthenics, karate, kung fu. He read comics about superheroes – especially Superman and Batman – with fervor, and binge-watched action movies endlessly. In the end, death surprised him with a winning judo hold.

Somebody Do Something!

Naturally I'm hurrying. I'm not counting tiles or cement blocks in the sidewalk, but yes, I am avoiding the stripes. The walls slide by quickly, and I'm constantly checking the clock in my memory. Needless to say, the sky is blue and the trees in the park are dazzling. Suddenly I believe I'm seeing a glow coming from the newborn grass, which the springtime is pushing up from under the rot of snow-covered, soot-blackened soil. Yes, the glow's coming from the brightness of the Sun. I check these things out with a quick glance, as I rush to get ahead of the woman in front of me who, every time I try to pass her, manages to block me. She just totters along, self-absorbed, has no idea I'm behind her on a tear and would willingly throttle her for walking so slowly, for ignoring the haste of people with places to go.

I review in my memory my day's to-do list, papers and folders I need to bring, letters, phone numbers, anything that needs to be handled. I go over my list of priorities for the day, ranking everything according to importance or whim. The sidewalks keep going by until finally I come to the mail drop, into which I hurl several letters and bills with all the violence possible in an act that takes a quarter of a second.

I enter the mouth of the Underworld. No sign of the crater or Lake Avernus, but the place's rules and inconveniences are posted, its annoyances known. For example, that we will suffer in the bowels of the earth for several long minutes is a given; we'll feel the hot breath of the underworld, its foul, motionless air that punctures the lungs; we'll witness its blackness that covers everything; those threads of water that trickle down the walls and make those bizarre stalactites. Then there's the station message board's notes to read, phrases jotted in pencil, or black or red crayon, quips, self-promotions, people entertaining themselves while they're locked in their own crystal balls, their tiny mental worlds, waiting for the train.

Suddenly someone calls attention to himself by casting a nervous glance around, eyes crammed with emptiness and crass surprise, scrutinizing the crowd. He then retreats into his warped plans for the day, his calculated steps to reach ultimate success, his tally of savings currently earning five and a half percent, his summer vacation. He sees holidays as the way to change personality, match the landscape – this year, maybe France, Holland, the Caribbean. Another sun, another language, time devoted to learning the sweetness of sloth.

The train's taking a suspicious amount of time. A giant clock pops up in the minds of the waiting creatures. How is this possible? More than five minutes' wait at rush hour! How can one deal with these trains? Workers forever asking for raises but never improving the service. Workers who earn more than we do, and still they complain. Workers who don't have to take the train to get to work early because they're sure to have a car. Workers who don't have to wait like flocks of dumb sheep. Workers in control. And passengers? "Let them take cabs, if they're in such a hurry!"

At last the train approaches, heralded by the cabalistic symbol on the engine, a lit-up letter of the Phoenician alphabet. The wheels' rubber coverings damp the noise as the train pulls in, exhaling puffs of chilled air through slits of the doors. The crowd takes the train by storm and forces all the cars' doors to remain open. The frenzy of conquest lights everybody's eyes, their barbaric passion spurred on by haste.

Inside, time comes to a halt and the empire of ads begins: computers, investment houses, cellphones, everything imaginable takes on ritualistic importance, every word has weight compounded by the crowd's enslavement to time. Everybody hides in thought, makes their faces expressionless, abandons lips that just hang there with obscene apathy, eyes emptied and muscles allowed to go flaccid, souls acceding to the dragon that advances breathing fire in the darkness under the buildings of New Babylon.

Fashion dictates are observed in passenger attire: articles made of Space cloth, blouses of tiny square mirrors, coats of sea-urchin spines, which, seen from a distance, are super-charged with sketchiness and very high style. Executives identifiable by their black and brown briefcases are further distinguishable into "old" and "up-and-coming" by certain gestures signaling that the brief-cases have well-deserved resting places in their owners' large offices with panoramic windows from which they can tame sky-scrapers with a glance; or else they demonstrate the aggressive ambition of young cubicle jockeys and occupants of open offices lacking any privacy. Somehow, they all appear willing to knock down anyone who stands in their way. Workers are further distin-guishable by types of fabric: polyester stands out among female secretaries and office assistants, while natural fibers like silk, wool, and linen identify executives of all sexes. Cotton, which the Egyp-tians say is going extinct, is secretly worn by all.

Before reaching Seventh Avenue, the train gently coasts to a halt. Expectation. No one dares ask what's going on. Everyone's confident that, whatever it is, it will be fixed. The problems that occupy our brains are more important, our plans for promotions, our maneuvers to give a little push to the person we want to re-place, our developing the art of doing as little as possible for the maximum result. The dream of the crowd invades everybody's eyelids and makes us squint helplessly, as old sleep tries to recover what we lost over the weekend.

A black man advances through the crowds in the cars. In his conductor's uniform, he's very dapper. This is as far as he's going – he's quitting, he says. He's not working a minute longer. He is done grinding all the live-long day for The Man. If work creates health, fine – give jobs to the sick.

"It's someone else's turn to take care of it!" he exclaims, laughs, then immediately disappears.

Huge clocks pop up in the minds of the crowd. At once, eve-rybody pictures the dreaded hour, nine A.M. All continue to work through in their minds how to save time when the train eventually pulls into their station: how to get around the old geezers, the lame on crutches, the wheelchair-bound, the one or two mothers and/or nannies on the way to day care with infants in strollers, who are now asking themselves what in the world made them imagine it would be a great idea to get a breath of fresh air and maybe go shopping.

How to sprint out of the elevator and avoid the boss's glare.

Nobody moves. Clearly something will happen.

EXPLORATION OF THE CLOSET

When I opened the closet door, I found a passageway. Without stopping to think, without describing the slots in the threshold or the cracks that branched out on the walls' surfaces, without pausing to read the name of the architect engraved boldly in stone with the words Anno Domini and the Roman numerals MCLXXVII, without thinking of the multiple distractions lurking there, I briskly walked in. The hall smelled damp, and as I proceeded, I began to have a funny feeling the sea was nearby. It was more of an impression, because I wasn't receiving the sea through my senses, or thinking about it; it was more an intuition of its presence, an exaggeratedly marine something accentuated in that passage. I went on, trying to keep my balance without jumping or stumbling. When I was quite far along, I could make out a huge square full of people waving flags and placards. I joined the crowd and saw the faces of the strange creatures that, unbeknownst to me, populated my closet. The spark of faith shone in their eyes: they were energetic and determined. Interestingly, everyone in that crowd was young and beautiful. I couldn't find even one senior or minor, or crippled, vision-impaired, or height-impaired individual. No, not a one – they were all young, beautiful, happy. I asked the person nearest me, "What's with this crowd?" The young woman, still smiling, exclaimed: "What? You don't know? We congregate to get charged with energy!" I thought I hadn't heard correctly and responded with more precision, "Excuse me please, but what is the purpose of this meeting?" "It's not a meeting, *chica,*" she said, slipping into Spanish, "*es una concentración para cargarnos de energía.*" Well okay then, I thought, they're getting all charged up with energy. At least that was clear. Now, off in the distance, I saw an ice-cream vendor. Fighting my way through the crowd to get to his cart, I asked for a sugar cone with plain chocolate ice cream. He said well, actually, he didn't have any ice cream; he was just decorative. It was refreshing to find him in this mob, representing the concept of ice-cream vendor without actually selling it. In the face of such an answer, I moved on. Since nobody was standing on the dais charging the throng with energy, I decided (contrary to my usual aversion to performing in public) that I would climb up there and improvise a speech that would galvanize the masses. But I couldn't move because the speaker had arrived and the crowd was automatically pushing me back to make way for him. The speaker jumped right in, addressing the crowd with this message: "From your common cold to your tuberculosis is just a single step! Avoid this and cure yourself with Acardet! Fortify your defenses with Acardet! Acardet, a product of Laso Laboratories!" The crowd broke out in wild applause. Everything dissolved into deepest darkness, with only a single light visible at the end, and as I headed towards it, I invoked the spirit of Alice, who had managed to survive in similar circumstances. The light came from a copper door that had torches strategically placed on either side of its threshold. I opened the door, telling myself, "This is a dream and, truly, nothing tragic can happen." That was when I found a gathering of European and Latin American intellectuals, deliberating which novel to choose as the best of the year, or so I imagined hearing from the lips of one of the members. Taking notice of my intrusion into the room, the intellectuals adjusted their glasses and asked me whom I represented. Briefly I narrated the history of the closet, but my defense (was it really a defense?) seemed a little lame. They repeated, "Who do you represent? The Third World?" To stop them from continuing to interrogate me, I answered that, truly, I represented the sea; after all, when I was transiting the passageway, it had felt like the sea. "You," said one of the award judges, "cannot represent the sea because you are not sufficiently marine. Come on, you don't even have gills!" Given this kind of logic, I replied that I was an observer. "Observer of whom? from which country? representing which collective of masses?" Somewhat irritated, I said that I was an observer of myself, of my own head, using my own eyes. Then they all stood up, accused me of being both fellow traveler and spy, and literally kicked me out of the room with their boots. So there I was, back at the copper door and surrounded by darkness. Was I a product of this corridor, I wondered, or was everything just my obsessive imagination? I plodded ahead through the darkness and at length found myself in a white room full of a numberless quantity of objects as diverse as small ashtrays, spools of thread, brandy snifters. The impression of being snowed under by small things made me flee to the other room, blue and bursting with even more objects. But among them were sea creatures, as well as actual sea. Since I had already figured out the significance of these things, I was not at all surprised that this sea did not get me wet. It was like the ice-cream man in the crowd: the concept of sea, not the sea itself. At that moment, floating on those nonexistent waves, because I wanted to wake up, instead, I fell asleep.

PARITY ACHIEVED

In a certain year of this millennium, on a blue and transparent afternoon, full of air not contaminated by radioactivity (far away were the radioactive darknesses distributed in the world during the Great Global War), of light reflected in pure and crystalline waters, in rivers whose fish of various colors jumped into the atmosphere, moved by the euphoria of the return to the origin; on that specific afternoon a peculiar object descended from the brilliance of the heavens.

Upon reaching the ground, it raised a circle of dust around it and then sank a few inches into the ground. The violence of its crash produced clouds of smoke from the propulsion system that spread languidly among the trees. The celestial object was a dodecahedron, green with red polka-dots not unlike a clown's costume. It remained stationary on the ground while its atoms shed the heat created by friction with the Earth's atmosphere. Inside the object, the crew set about repairing the ship's brain, the Ball of Destiny, a species of electronic brain and horoscope in the form of a divinatory ball that contains all events past and present, but also of the future. This ball was indistinguishable from one that had long ago belonged to a capricious Chinese empress and which may still be seen at the Penn Museum in Philadelphia. Before the reader starts whining about this being cultural nonsense, it should be said that such a ship and its devices defied all our ideas of what a space capsule should be. Both the celestial object and its crew represented The Other, alien to the nth degree.

Inside the capsule, the creatures, who had wanted to go to the Andromeda galaxy because its oval shape gave them a sense of security, had fallen by mistake into the Milky Way, whose stellar tentacles horrified them. So they consulted the intergalactic navigation books while they (another curiosity) took tea sitting at a round table. It was astounding that they should practice a tea ceremony, just as the Japanese do still to this day. The ship had fallen in Nixoniana, a country broken off from the one-time United States and named in honor of the disgraced F-A-P (Former-American-President) Richard Milhous Nixon, he who created the "Hispanic" and "Asian" races now making up the majority of the nation's population – and he whom the Chinese worshipped because of Nixon's fateful trip to China, which ultimately led to the collapse of the world economy, through no fault of the Chinese.

While the aliens ceremoniously drank their tea, outside the ship a large crowd dedicated its excited conversations to speculating what that object that seemed to have escaped from a circus might be. This standoff went on until the Destiny Ball inside the ship was repaired and ordered the aliens to open the hatch and step outside: it was time to introduce themselves to the inhabitants of the third planet from the Sun. Following that order, they opened the hatch and came out.

Seeing the crew materialize from inside the space object, the earthlings took a step back. "What grotesquely anarchic beings!" was the gist of what they murmured to one another, because these creatures defied the law of universal parity. One half of each body was completely different from the other half, lacking even the remotest trace of bilateral symmetry. When observing such a geometric disaster, the earthlings were unable to suppress their displeasure and confusion. Not that they were such lovers of geometry, but their innate respect for convention was, put simply, uncontrollable. Their peculiar concept of right and left, of proportion and parity, would not allow them to conceive of an order within disorder. Earthlings could not understand a hegemony of the odd, of the unequal, of the different. Not even the fauna of the Cambrian, those strange forms that looked as if an art director were learning how to design and draw, could be compared.

Faced with these beings from another world that demanded so much cognitive and classifying power, the humans gave up. And what was even more curious, they could not actually see the visitors because their brains had no concepts to explain them, something like what happened to the Caribbean Indians when Spanish ships first anchored in their bays. The Indians continued to live their normal lives without noticing that they had great nautical structures in front of them: as they lacked the concepts to understand them, they therefore could happily ignore them (until it was too late). In the same way, the earthlings could not really see those intergalactic beings and decided to go back home and ignore what had happened.

By contrast, the intergalactics experienced a strange new emotional shock: boredom. The repetition of the parts, the imitation of the halves, immersed them in a universe of geometric speculations and plastic possibilities, which resulted in concrete tedium. Fortunately for them, while parity might be boring to observe, it was tasty to eat. Once they discovered that the earthly ones were delicious, the anarchic beings organized regular bacchanalia where the most roly-poly of human specimens were served. They were so tactful about this that the leftover (thin) human specimens never came to know anything about these events.

Thanks to the nutritional convenience of this new planet, the aliens settled in without difficulty. And, although they committed what some might consider atrocities, these paled by comparison with the new epidemics of cholera, bubonic plague, and sundry evolving viruses that had to be addressed constantly, like forest fires. So, humankind lived with these creatures in the same way that from the beginning of history, they have lived with everything else that irritated them, having to either recognize it or combat it. Meanwhile, the asymmetrical beings, now regularly feeding their bodies with fatal parity, gradually began to reconcile their halves, almost becoming unities in the mirror.

WOOD

The atmosphere had the pinkish tinge that characterizes certain rainy afternoons; but it could be said that this particular transparency, this lightness of air, this mysterious floating among the leaves that gradually invaded the surroundings, struck an unsettling note and presented an expressiveness inaccessible to those of limited sensibility.

The leaves filled the streets: leaves the color of tin, of thick, molten copper, glowing alarmingly, and yet one sensed that the leaves were allowing themselves something like a show of strength, offering a kind of glimpse into their world with faintly malevolent compassion.

Surrounded by leaves, the house shone in the pearly autumn twilight. Yes, a beautifully built house on a promontory, it was surrounded by equal houses, built on smaller headlands. The house, of common appearance except for giving the impression of a bastion of medieval princes, seemed to resemble all the others, but the slight tremor that shook its impeccably painted white walls suggested that its lack of uniqueness was just camouflage.

In the portal of the house, a teenage girl was playing quietly with a ball. Composed of water and reflections, the ball kept its shape by who knows what miracle of cohesion. I contemplated the girl, the ball, and the house, which still throbbed with amiable expressiveness, as if to signal that my own affectless reaction to what I was looking at was deliberate.

I approached the teenager with the sharp-edged ball and the deadly reflexes. I spoke to her without fussing about grammar or etymological correctness in my word choice or pronunciation. I spoke to her the way torrents roar and waterfalls shriek. The girl showed her good manners by only changing the color of her eyes while, like nature in agony, my discourse went on.

By the time my rant was over, the girl's ball had turned into a timid frog peeking out of its mistress's left ear, where it had clearly decided to hide for the duration. The girl did not laugh. Despite her extreme youth, she knew the great danger she might expose herself to by letting her guard down at that moment when the most powerful planetary forces were aligning and could make everything explode in less than a minute (the Sun was in grim opposition with five planets in Scorpio, including Uranus, creator of sudden changes, and Pluto, shaker of the unconscious mind).

Suddenly, she quickly said her name, which was not new to me, since I remembered dreaming it one afternoon while sleeping under the benevolent shadow of an orange tree. Her name was Wood. Yes, she said her name – Wood, exactly, the English word *wood* – and at once went back to playing with her ball, to prove that she hadn't stopped being a normal person, that her name was no cause for wonder.

Wood became impatient and spoke in an informal way, using disjointed words that seemed not to belong to any known language. She seemed rather to invent words, along with the ideas they represented, to show her desire to effect change in the world of the abstract and the concrete. Only later did she dare use coherent phrases, when she was not afraid of being betrayed by ears that did not listen, or that misunderstood. Wood spoke of the image of the Eternal State, and wanted to demonstrate her competence in such matters when she handed me her vision of the inscrutable monster that others called Leviathan.

Wood imagined the State as a Vedic beast having multiple heads and thousands of arms spinning in a macabre oriental dance. The hands of the State were armed with daggers, and razor-sharp death would not keep people waiting. Wood knew we were returning from a strange dream that was anything but pleasant.

And now, putting on the physiognomy of the state, with hundreds of prying police eyes and numberless rivers of tears flowing down her cheeks, thanks to the apostates of the Supreme Science of Necessary Evil, Wood seems a sphinx eager to be covered up by the cunning desert sands.

She shows her Mediterranean heritage via a certain adaptability to the landscape: by merging with her ball, ensconcing herself in her house's walls, speaking with gestures that seem to rely more on shape than on concept. Thus, little by little, through the fissures that proceed to open up in disparate planes or worlds of existence, as our communication progresses, there comes a moment when everything spins around and intermingles. Nearby promontories become interwoven, houses penetrate one another, leaves become confounded with the house's bricks: everything gradually becomes a compact mass of multiple colors and shades, until it becomes difficult to distinguish between my hands and the roots of trees or the paintings by Max Ernst that Wood stores in the attic of her house.

THE MAN IN THE BLACK FEDORA HAT

I was headed into the movie theater at the same time that the tall, thin man with the broad-brimmed black fedora hat was leaving. This hat had a lustrous silk band with a small red feather tucked into its flat bow. I bumped into him. He disintegrated into a flock of crows that instantly flew off.

Sitting very close to the movie screen, I knew I had to develop enough retinal retention to see certain freeze-frames of Ingmar Bergman's *Persona* because an urgent message was going to be given to me. I had to see the instant as time without end and decode it. All the other moviegoers would have to be blind to the frames; otherwise, afterwards they might develop deep anxiety or suicidal depression, never realizing what they had seen.

An erect penis with hairy testicles flashes by in a fraction of a second on the screen. Is this the message? Sex as the source of life? Sex as the path to enlightenment? Maybe my dreams will give me a clue.

That night I dream that I visit the cats' fountain in the nearby park. The man with the fedora hat is standing in the middle of the park's narrow, winding road with several cats in his arms. One of them, a black one, jumps down and walks towards me. His fur is marbled with white, brown, and beige hairs. He's not black at all; instead, his coat is made up of many changing colors. The cat sits down in front of me, raises his head and looks at me with very intelligent and loving blue eyes.

"You have chosen me, so I choose you," I say, picking him up.

My hands have photographic ability: they retain the imprint of things I touch. I set the cat on the ground, but the cat's image is still on my hands: a past my hands are still attached to, and do not want to let go, the way we must do when we spring up into the world of the spirit and the body falls down into the world of death and the grave.

I wake up with great thirst. When I turn on the bathroom faucet, glowing red strawberries spill into the oval white ceramic sink bowl. I go to the kitchen and open a bottle of mineral water. When I try to drink it, the water backs up into the bottle. Maybe I want it too much. I'm too thirsty. I try again with less intensity and finally coax the water out of the bottle into my dry mouth. There's an art to this, I think. A way of approaching things, sort of like moving gracefully with your partner in the ballroom.

My apartment's too hot. I open a window and a cold, apple-scented breeze waltzes into the room, cooling it a few degrees. I look down. Under a street lamp, still lit in this early foggy morning hour, the man in the black fedora hat looks up at me and winks. I'm offended. I feel he is making me an accomplice in some past debauchery, like he remembers seeing me in some seedy whorehouse but is not going to tell my wife.

A toothache makes me shut my eyes in pain. When I open them again the man in the black fedora hat is flying in front of my window. He has no wings, just seems unaffected by gravity. He floats like a cloud and disappears among the skyscrapers like a child's balloon.

LINEAR A

I wake up feeling my entire body crawling with ants. I touch my-self. My hands perceive not insects but letters freshly tattooed on my skin. I run to see my body in the bathroom mirror. It's entirely covered with mysterious black symbols. The ink's still not dry, but it doesn't smudge my fingers.

Last night I went to a bar and stayed till all hours. I drank God knows how many beers with a firefighter who had just left his wife and wanted me to grant him absolution. I'm no priest, but I tried to help him rationalize his action. He thanked me with one free round of ale after another.

"There is nothing better than a beer when you leave your roots and escape up the roof."

"Is that what you did?"

"That's what the angel would have said. He could come again any time now."

MISTAKE

At the most intense moment of the film, the blond man in my row gets up from his seat and, as he walks past me, steps on my operated foot. Blind with pain, I pull out the gun I'm carrying tucked in my belt and shoot him in the head. The blond man collapses, his brains, white and gray, splattering across the red carpet of the theater. I get up and run down the aisle to the theater's side door, ignoring the audience's horrified cries. A block from the cinema, I turn around and see the blond man running after me, almost catching up with me. Full of terror, I lift my hand to my chest when a pain that feels like the point of a dagger penetrates my heart. I collapse panting, and curl up on the pavement. The blond man stoops to bring his face close to mine, to see me more clearly. "How have you been resurrected? I blew your brains out!" I say, feeling the pain in my heart. "Not me – my identical twin brother," says the blond man, cruelly. His smile is the last thing I see before I leave my body.

THE UNIFIER'S MISSION

I

"Soggr, I am not setting foot inside that lampfish," I say in jest, trying to diffuse the intensity of its energy. I can't calculate the lampfish's distance from me without the appropriate instruments, but that doesn't make the slightest difference because it's is as fast as it is remote, and I will lose my shadow before I agree to step inside it.

"Unifier, it is easy for you to negate. Think before launching your words into the atmosphere."

"True, my refusals in the past have had some – shall we say – negative repercussions. So, why don't we see what happens this time when – "

I was going to say "I adamantly refuse to interfere!" but Soggr the Enforcer is this type of intergalactic entity who appears sometimes as an opalescent gaseous being, and at others as a frequency, but in both manifestations Soggr thinks in eleven registers at once. You get one specific answer only because it happens to be the one in the slot of its cloudy mouth when you try to weasel out of something.

And so fortuitously it says, "NOOOO! You can't retract your words once they are in space. Inscribed in it they are." Soggr's intense anxiety turns him into a flash of speeding rainbow light which can be seen only from the corner of the eyes. Corners? Depends on the number of eyes....

"What is a 'word' to you, Enforcer?" I ask, laughing at Soggr's seriousness.

I turn to admire the smallest of our seven suns diving into the horizon with a green and violet splash. A sudden fine rain of reflective jewels projects the light onto the incandescent mauve of our volcanic-sulfur clouds, suffusing their borders with a musky rose tone. Purple lightning flashes traverse the clouds horizontally and branch out in multiple red filaments.

A threatening register rotates into Soggr's cloudy mouth. "Unifier, you know that you have been assigned extrapolation."

"Aha!" I exclaim mockingly, combining Soggr's words like obedient amino acids and turning them, by extreme pressure, into peptides. "In that case my power to speak and live must be gone."

The jewel rain ceases. Our largest sun is rising, and its white rays on my welcoming skin turn my legs more intensely purple and shiny, and their pores emit a more phosphorescent green. Dayflower bulbs burst into leaves and blossoms in the ultraviolet-saturated soil, and, exploding, send their multicolored seeds into the air. Where they land, new bulbs swell out and plunge roots into the soil, and in another moment more flowers materialize, honeybees swarm in for the nectar, then pollinate still other flowers, in the whirlwind of seven suns a day, each radiating a different kind of light.

Soggr is masked in a fog created by coughing gently – such a struggle to reach the register of sycophancy. "What I mean is, you will not talk and live in your most suitable frame. Please, of the lampfish think, and Unifier be gone. It is the judgment."

"The judgment of beings with too much jocularity and very little common sense."

Soggr makes a growling sound of exasperation. "The Council of Clowns sends you to extrapolation. Unifier, unify you must."

"Say no more, Enforcer. I really don't have time for the opinion of those jokers." I surprise Soggr by entering the lampfish and, in one deft movement, departing at the speed of thought.

II

The lampfish's speed opens up a tunnel in the nearest black region. Its skin's frictionless slime fends off the infinite waves of disintegration and causes them to pinch us through, squirting us out the other side into the flat, bumpy, leaky mother universe. This explodes in our field of vision as a flash of white light. Now, the lampfish must negotiate the black, non-sticky jelly blobs at the slower speed of dreams, giving me a chance to sip energy from the light projected by a minute, almost domesticated sun that floats, spinning directly in front of me, inside its own force field. Through the lampfish's transparent membranes, this tiny sun seems to be inside a gold cage hanging from a ceiling.

I am not entirely reassured by the lampfish's transformation into a lens showing this universe to be very similar to mine, where great dumb agglutinant invisible matter encroaches and flows around small, congealed, visible bits, such as us.

We swim among colorful nebulae and clusters, nomad galaxies colliding and flinging luckless stars into the exile of empty space. I begin to enjoy the trip when I see stars pop into existence and snuggle in gas-rich spirals.

But then we run into next-to-nonexistent star formation in the gas-poor ellipticals, and I become despondent. Still, the show is impressive: galaxies cradling countless binary stars with rocky and gaseous planets orbiting them; here and there the occasional solitary star festooned with planets; odds and ends of stars slung out of their galaxies by supermassive black holes into velvet blackness, with their orbiting planets struggling uncomfortably to keep up. Well done, I think, at the sight of red hyper giants that explode into iron, calcium, and other heavy elements; of the massive globs of gold, along with gamma rays, splattering away from colliding neutron stars; of more novas and supernovas and gigantic hungry black holes in the centers of galaxies, burping evermore gamma rays from their poles; then, errant, small black holes like tiny mouths, sipping distractedly at helpless planets and hot glowing gases; the cadavers of massive stars some call pulsars, as well as magnetars, or magnetic neutron stars, aging with discreet dignity; red, brown, black, and white dwarfs; diamond stars rotating with no memory of their radiant youth; planets large and small revolving around enormous or diminutive suns. I see runaway rebel planetary couples obsessively orbiting each other in the darkness of interstellar and intergalactic space; lonely hypervelocity planets cruelly ripped from their stars by monstrous black holes and flung at almost the speed of light from their galaxies; dwarf planets, remnants of the formation of their systems, wandering around their suns in opaque grey belts; frozen satellites skulking, immersed in frigid ice, and rocky ones disfigured by craters from millions of meteorites crash-landing on them; adventurous comets flying here and there, following long, lonely, sometimes erratic orbits; sociable asteroids commuting in bands, doing loops around their local star; rings of chunks of ice and rock going around gaseous giants; then, what looks like space, huge with luminous blobs of plasma, stellar winds, frigid gases, all the detritus and dust of stars and planetary material propelled in space by my erstwhile friend, the funny dividing force.

How galling it must be! The Divider can't stop every sphere from rotating around its own axis, satellites from orbiting around their planets, planets around their stars, and stars around their galaxies. Even more galling, in fact extremely frustrating to the Divider, is that the constantly changing red, green, and blue clouds of hydrogen, helium, nitrogen, and the other ionized elements emitting purple, violet, pink, and golden light, just keep giving birth to stars of two to five prongs. In this particular universe there are no nice, bright quasars, although if I look back in spacetime there used to be. Clearly, this is an issue: where are there any objects of extreme luminosity, at the centers of very active galaxies, near supermassive, frantically spinning black holes? Did the Council of Clowns ask me if I'd rather live here in this universe, so much older than my baby one that's full of superclusters of quasars? Noo! The whole lot of the Clowns haven't the power to confront the Divider in this universe with its endless reddish galaxies that have stopped producing suns and are crammed full of red stars: red and dead. Only a fool would trade this wealth of heavy elements for my baby universe's crystal bluish galaxies that are constantly creating new blue giants – all those hot young stars.

"Enough of repetition!" I say. "This universe is older, but it is based on the same boring light and heavier elements. I want something new." Rethink this concept? – in light of what my mission is?

I tell the lampfish's instruments to give me a graphic of what exists beyond this universe. The instruments laugh. This rude reaction makes me realize it's time to take charge. "Lampfish, resist the pull to move either to the right or the left following the electromagnetic skin of this mother universe, and puncture its spacetime!" It's time I let the instruments hear my command voice.

The lampfish obligingly dives through the carapace of this expanding, dying universe and plunges into the uncreated unknown, the nothingness that can't be thought.

There are times – not many, but enough – when I can be, well, gullible. Behold a single, solitary white dwarf, a diamond star, the crystallized carbon core of a sun that has burned up all its fuel. Thanks for the heads up, Lampfish, I think sarcastically, and feel the lampfish wag its tail in response. The jewel captures what light there is and sparkles in the darkest of darkness. It rings like a giant gong, a disturbing, pulsating tone which I can hear through the soundwaves translator.

This type of star exists all over the mother universe, even clearer and more brilliant; sometimes they pass as stars because their shining facets reflect the changing red, blue, gold, violet of the nearest suns' thermal glow.

The only thing different about this dwarf star is that it's falling – and so are we. Nothing falls in the mother and the child universes, thanks to their conscious, living, palpitating, floating fibers and warps that hold everything in place. But here, there are no warps left, only what seems like a hungry abyss, into which we have started to plunge at alarming speed.

Having arrived at the place the Clowns apparently intend me to be, the lampfish vomits me out and bolts back to the mother universe, fleeing to its transportation aquarium in the fifth dimension. On the white dwarf, free of the lampfish, I walk over the tender crystalline ground enveloped in my portable atmosphere. Although it sticks to me like an undetectable halo, it's actually produced by the diamond star, whose milky atmosphere is not breathable, but grains of silver light still emanate from the core of the star through diamantine, flexible tubes, bounce back from the chalky sky, and shower my body like jewels. If they bother me when they hit my head, I just have to raise my hand for them to turn into flowers. But these weak photons offer little fodder to my photosynthesizing pores, so to increase their power I shout a sound frequency that optimizes the production of energy in my cells.

I sense a presence. My peripheral vision picks up a flashing opalescent light with unfortunate characteristics that remind me of Soggr. "It's a big disappointment having traveled through two universes to find these silly tricks," I shout in complaint to the entire star. "If you turn out to be Soggr, I promise my screams will shatter this whole star."

I sense a movement.

"It's your own creation," says a high-pitched voice like little tinkling bells. "Your mind is giving you a logical interpretation. You'll go mad if you really see us. How will you be able to understand something completely different?"

"Hah! Soggr, the Enforcer in my universe, is an intergalactic essence. Maybe he escaped from this rogue star."

"Soggr we acknowledge as a composite of our lackadaisical moods which we let loose in your universe. We intended that he should be captured by the gravitational force of your planet. We also created – only the abyss can really create – your mother and, afterward, your daughter universe. That last one was our best so far, but it's still capricious and erratic."

"What was your point?" I ask testily.

"What purpose? Just a flowering of our minds. Pure enjoyment of energy."

"And I suppose the Council of Clowns is your idea of entertainment."

"The Council of Clowns is the fruit of seeds we planted in your planet, a natural development. Your extrapolation was our idea."

"Why?"

"Among other things, we are lonely."

"How many of you are there?"

"Oh, myriads."

"How can you be lonely?"

"We all know the same things; we are as one. It's like being a flower with an infinite number of petals. Like universes."

"What? Are there even more universes?"

"Innumerable, but they were created by the previous batches, the Resters who now think that creation is frivolity. They also created the parallel universes, but that's not my department. Their main creator (you may think this is your friend the Divider, but no) believed in richness, multiplicity, variety, excess. Everything that can be thought, should exist, be improved, and flourish. She connected them through gravity and went crazy, of course. We, who believe in economy and simplicity, created the last two; those you know, as I just said.

"The mother universe had a difficult beginning because at first, we were no good at designing. The first animals we invented were really ugly, but we learned and refined our artistic abilities. Engineering was also important to make everything work flawlessly – we learned with practice.

"Still, the explosions are rather crude. We are working on creating heavy elements more elegantly, and also multiplying them following a more ingenious plan. Also, the biological stuff is still complicated and mechanistic – you might say, clunky."

"In my opinion, the big problem is the heavy elements. Nothing but trouble there!" I had my reasons for thinking this. They were the ultimate cause of my trip.

"Yes, well, we may be in a bit of a rut there, but where would we be with only splashes of colors and wise music?"

"If you don't mind my asking – why is your star falling?"

"It is *not* falling. It is pirouetting." – This spoken with a certain arrogant testiness.

This is pure semantics, I thought, but realizing my situation, I quickly put the idea out of my head and asked, "Where are you pirouetting to?"

"To the planet Ocean, in the mother universe. We will get there in the blinking of an eye in an envelope of electromagnetic energy designed to protect you. One of their inhabitants is about to unglue our handiwork and turn that universe into a grave of hydrogen. Which will infect all the other universes. You are to help us avoid this."

"Why me?"

"Because you are visible, Unifier. You can communicate with the Oceanities without spooking them."

III

I am unaware of our transit between those last words of the diamond beings until I see before me a black planet full of small white and yellow points of light. I scream to produce atmosphere because I feel I am about to faint.

"Stop that ghastly sound! Here, consume this solar flower!"

A beautiful yellow flower appears and I absorb energy from its fiery petals. I can think again and relax.

"What is this planet of blackness? How can its inhabitants live in this darkness?"

"Calm down… we are on the night side of it. Their only young sun is on the other side; a rarity in this universe of mostly binary stars. To create a solar flower to feed you at night, just think of the Sun and it will appear. You now have this power. You can also take with you your portable atmosphere. You have six biological compounds in your genetic code whereas the planet's inhabitants have only four.

"You also lack guanine, or marine-bird excrement, so you are an improvement, an upscale model of the younger universe. Besides, your civilization is older than theirs so you have more resources physically and mentally. Your mirror neurons will transform your body to sort of look like them. Understand and speak their gibberish by raising your mind to the universal wavelength. It will not be perfect, though. You are not that developed yet. Try not to attract attention. And be humble. You will have available to you unfamiliar vocabulary and phenomena, as well as concepts as exotic as gender. You will automatically understand their clichés. Now, jump into the electromagnetic pod and once you arrive, look for a red-haired child. It will lead you to the creature who is creating the problem."

The Active One circles me at great speed producing all the colors of the rainbow and a rumbling sound of pregnant methane clouds. I fall gracefully in space towards this sunless part of the planet Ocean.

IV

"Why do you glow so much?" says a creature in a pink body covering. The Sun is now shining. The creature is picking up shells on the beach.

"Oh, I must have drunk a very potent Sun ray!" I say, smiling, and admiring its shining gold hair. "I will adjust my inner dimmer." I mentally order my Reflectin proteins to lower their iridescence.

I look at the sparkling, mouth-watering turquoise sea, the scintillating, succulent azure sky and I start to salivate, a throwback to when our mouths were used to eat.

"What a delectable Sun you have here! So mellifluous and honey-like!" I say, sticking out my tongue and licking the air.

"Where are you from?" asks the creature cautiously.

"Oh, from out-of-town. I have a very active imagination."

"Really. I never met anybody like you."

"And I have never met anybody like you either."

"My school is full of kids like me." Pause. "Except they're really not."

"Ahah! I would have to see kids to understand what you mean. Is there anything about me that you would like to change? I don't want to be too different."

The kid laughs, and suddenly they are conspirators. "Actually, you look okay, but I wouldn't run around in that scuba-diving outfit if I were you. I can give you sandals, old pants and a work shirt of my father's. He won't notice. He barely knows what day it is, he's so into his work."

V

I am walking on the sidewalk, exploring this beach town now that I'm properly dressed.

Suddenly, a larger kid runs out of a house across the street and a moment later a grown version of this kid runs out of the house as well.

"Have you seen Mark?" it screams at me.

"I don't know what is mark. How does it look like?" I shout.

"Mark is a red-haired little boy!"

I look around and see "red-haired little boy – Mark" – hiding behind a tree. Covered with red on top and light brown on the bottom (the diamantine translator tells me this garb is khaki shorts and a red t-shirt), Mark is jumping up and down with excitement, holding the tree trunk with both hands.

"There," I signal with a finger. "Behind that tree."

"Thanks!"

Mark emerges from behind the tree making violent gestures. The adult form runs and catches the boy.

"Want to come in? Have a drink? You look … new in town," says the adult form with a smile, holding Mark.

I cross the street and the adult form – finally the vocabulary kicks in, and I know he is a "man" with gendered pronouns, he, him, his – extends his right hand. I tentatively do the same and I'm momentarily terrified as he grasps me briefly.

"I'm Neil," he says in a friendly tone.

"I'm Candra," I answer imitating his intonation and gestures.

"Weird name."

"Yes, I am from the other side of the sky."

"You mean India."

"Sort of," I say, not knowing what he means.

"C'mon in. It's too hot outside."

VI

"Liz, this is Candra, from India," Neil says to the kid in pink I saw earlier this morning, sitting now on a wicker sofa in the living room.

Looking up from a black tablet with a colored screen, the kid seems surprised.

"He's Indian? Wow! I thought he was a Cuban rafter."

"Liz!"

"I met him at the beach. I was picking shells. I gave him some old clothes of yours."

"You know what happens to trusting little girls and boys around the country. They are kidnapped and become sex slaves for organized crime," he whispers, thinking I can't hear him. I have no idea what he is talking about.

"You can see perfectly well he is disorganized and not a criminal," Liz says definitively.

"Because she is a child prodigy, she thinks she knows everything," Neil tells me, irritation mixed with pride in his voice as he nods toward Liz.

"Well, Liz knew me," I say, and somehow, I realize it is true.

Neil goes to the kitchen and returns with two clinking small glasses with ice cubes and a golden liquid inside.

"Here is to your health," he says drinking and offering me the other glass. I imitate the way he drinks without drinking and put the glass on a little table beside a chair. The kids say "good night" and leave the room, and Neil and I sit on wicker chairs. I select the one near my drink, but don't touch it.

"What brings you to this beach town?" he asks nicely, but I can tell he is sorry he invited me into his house not knowing who I am.

I look at him and I don't know what to answer. He notices my embarrassment and smiles.

"Listen, if you really are illegal, I won't denounce you. Do you know science? All the Indians I've known have been very good with science and mathematics. They all want to live in big cities, or I would hire them for my project."

How easy this is turning out to be. "Yes, of course I know science and mathematics. I would be glad to be of help."

Unfortunately, my willingness puts him off. "Well, maybe. We have a shack in the backyard and you can stay there for a while. I'll figure something you can do to help out – mow the lawn (if we had any, with this drought!), clear the beach of storm debris, check on the turtle egg nests – you'll feel useful."

The shed is crammed to its tin roof with plenty of junk to build something to sleep on.

And of course there are tall stacks of exotic materials directly useful in this emergency, though Neil probably expects to use them for the opposite purpose.

VII

"You need to quit this chummy thing with these beings! You are here to stop this creature's experiments!"

The last thing I ever expect to hear, especially when I am sound asleep on a planet in a distant galaxy, is the Active One screaming in my ear. I'm in the shack. It's the middle of the night and I've been put to sleep by an incessant drone of insects, frogs, waves splashing on the beach – each sound carries with it a moving picture of what it looks like, and, as none seemed life-threatening, I fell asleep. They suddenly stop, as if they hear the Active One yelling at me, and then go back to making noise after I receive the message. I am very hungry. I've had to refuse everything I've been offered, and now they must think I'm fasting. I'll die if I eat their food. I can't digest it. I think about the Sun and the solar flower appears. Sipping its energy, I calm down and can get back to sleep again.

VIII

After taking a delicious sunbath and graciously refusing breakfast, I accompany Neil on the drive to his laboratory in the middle of town. Striding towards the elevator he says with enthusiasm:

"My idea is to split the gluons, the particles, or the flex tubes that some people describe as carrying the strong nuclear force that keeps the quarks together in the atomic nucleus. Of course, there are plenty of physicists who say gluons are fundamental particles and can't be divided, but the ancient Greeks said the same thing about atoms, and you know what happened when we split highly enriched uranium. We had the atomic bomb."

I can tell from his tone that this was something very destructive. He is projecting his concern. We stop in front of the elevator and Neil presses the up button.

"Are you sure this experiment is safe?"

"Well, once we split the gluons that hold the protons together, and keep the gluons separate, they'll repulse each other because they have the same positive energy and will break the atoms. We'll contain this breaking of atoms, of course, but we can weaponize it and aim it at enemy targets."

A curse on those Clowns. This is the kind of intervention I have said no to forever. It's pointless to chase around after worlds that have started on their path to destruction. It's always been my philosophy not to stop them: from their ruins something else, maybe better, always comes.

One day the survivors will learn about the self-destroyers, see the remains, find out why, and stop. For sure, lately when this has happened, I have sensed the hand of the Divider. In this splitting of gluons especially.

"Umm," I say, temporizing, "I was working on something like this in India and I think this is not an experiment that can easily be contained."

Neil gets a strange look on his face and moves his hand to a different button in the elevator. "Oh, let's go to my office instead of the lab and you can tell me all about it."

His office is on the top floor of this glass building of ten floors. The view of the city and the sea in the distance is beautiful. Neil sits down behind a large glass desk, and I sit in front of him in a very comfortable brown leather and metal chair, looking out at the town's rooftops and the sea in the distance. On the wall there are pictures of Neil holding hands with important-looking humans.

"I can't tell you everything because it's classified, I said. "But when we did computer simulations, we discovered in various experiments that the gluons carry a force that is connected throughout the universe. We were going to create a large isolated container to try it out, but even the smaller simulations were quite conclusive." I refrained from telling him we named the force "love."

"Are you saying gluons are entangled? Splitting them will provoke a reaction that will 'unglue' the whole of creation?"

"Something like that."

"How did you do the computer simulation?"

"You don't have the computers for it."

Now suspicion narrows Neil's eyes. "Did someone give you permission to contact me?"

"Yes – well, more of a mission to find you."

"Who did? This project is top secret."

"I can't say, but I was extrapolated because of this."

"You mean exiled?"

"Not exactly. It means, if I don't stop or kill you, I can't go home."

"How do I know you were not sent to stop me so India will make the discovery before the US?"

"That's impossible. But I can show you we are more advanced than you. Also, not only we, but others, have this knowledge."

I visualize the Sun, and the solar flower appears floating in front of Neil's face. I sip its rays through my skin. Neil opens his mouth, not believing his own eyes.

"Will this satisfy you?" I could do more tricks to convince him, but I sense he is already nearly losing his mind.

"Yes. But look, I was hoping to get the Nobel Prize for this discovery. I have backers, investors, government grants – I can't simply stop work based on what you are telling me. Piles of money have been spent on this research, with the idea that much bigger piles of money can be made from it. I'll have to discover something equally important that will satisfy everybody and not ruin me."

I look at him at a loss. *Ruin* him? Ruin *him*? If only. Though he seems well meaning enough…

"I know Indians can live many months without drinking and eating, but I know of no one who can get nourishment directly from the Sun. You are not Indian, are you?"

"No."

"What are you?"

"I am a conscious, intelligent being."

"I mean, where do you really come from?"

"From another universe."

"Yeah – not from another planet or galaxy, but from another *universe*," he says sarcastically.

"That's right."

"And I'm supposed to believe that?"

"It's the truth."

The Active One is suddenly screaming in my ear. "Quit pussy-footing around with this man! Kill him! Terminate at once this insane 'experiment'!"

"Kill him?" I think at the Active One. "You have no morals. How can I deprive the kids of their father?"

"Would you have all the fathers of the universe killed?"

"Morality is not quantitative."

"In our universe it is!"

"You sent the wrong being. You needed an assassin, not a Unifier!"

"I know what I need. You just don't want to do the job. Traveling through other universes has made you weak in the head. It's either him or you. Decide."

"Now, that's unfair. I will not be bullied. I won't submit to pressure. I have free will."

"You seem more of a demon than a creator! Invent something! You are more developed than they are – give them a better toy! I want results!"

The Active One lets out another frantic shriek again before disappearing in a whirlwind of fire.

None of this altercation can be seen or heard by Neil, who has started to type on his computer, but I cause the electricity to fail. What he calls a power outage is a good enough excuse to call it a day.

IX

"You will stop development on this gluon project now," I tell Neil in my command voice the next morning while he is having breakfast. I have been busy all night, compressing the work of centuries into seconds. "In place of it, you will discover – *today* – a weapon that will send a ray that temporarily paralyzes your enemies. Here are draft drawings, lists of materials, all easily accessible right here, most of it in your shed. In fact, your beach sand is particularly appropriate for glazing the reflective arrays you'll need to build. This weapon can only be used defensively. In that box you will find what your people call an expediter to speed up production. And speed is imperative."

I push across the breakfast table a box and the list of material I have spent the whole dark part of day forging out of junk in Neil's shack, along with other stuff expropriated from nearby habitations, using data and formulas I stripped out of Neil's computer yesterday while we were talking in his office. Much of what he's already done can be repurposed. Rays, after all, are rays, thermonuclear energy, cryo-nuclear energy, light, whatever. Lasers, for example, have been around doing good or evil on this planet for quite some time, but lasers and split gluons are not even close to being the same thing. It's the magnitude of what they can do to living beings that drastically differentiates them.

Neil has been deceived by his investors into thinking other cultures on his planet are behind in developing split-gluon ray generators. In fact, they already have large contraptions – whatever these perpetually hostile creatures call their machines – designed to spray Neil's country as revenge for centuries of meddling. I must force Neil to design and build attractor-deflectors for the split-gluon ray, to draw split-gluon streams to them and re-direct them in a debilitated state back to their points of origin.

The ray deflector that Neil is "on the verge of discovering" (if I've come in time) encapsulates the path of the original ray, creating something like a tunnel or a monorail and, without slowing the ray's velocity, redirects the energy back to its point of ignition, using this debilitated cryo-nuclear beam to temporarily freeze communication between neurons in the brain without permanent damage (hypothetically – this outcome is not certain).

No matter the split-gluon rays' points of origin – in one case the return must go to the Earth's satellite, the so-called Moon – the rays are constrained by rules of sub-molecular reciprocity when striking the reflector, thus preserving enough momentum to "get home."

"Like a boomerang, hm? We use reflected energy from gluon scission to return to its point of origin following its original trajectory? In the short time the energy takes to return to where it started from, it won't explode hearts or burst capillaries – it'll be harmless, other than making cognition temporarily unfeasible."

Neil is dumbfounded, so I say, "What you'll tell your investors is that you've conclusively proved that the gluon is really a fundamental particle that, once divided, seeks to return to its place of origin and reunite with itself. In truth, it's the foundation of the unified field that permeates the universe and keeps matter together. You can break it apart, but given the right focal arrays – don't shake your head, yes, *you* can build these, they are not complicated – it easily returns to its origin, and happily reunites and reconstitutes as gluon particles, giving its molesters a hefty slap in the face."

Expressionless, Neil stares at the pile of documents and prototypes on the glass desk in front of him. I can see his forehead over the pile: it is like a moving picture. He is thinking, and I can hear, "Alien operative," as, one by one, a slide show of cities with onion domes, minarets, or gigantic skyscrapers shrouded in dirty clouds flashes across the blank space over his eyes. One of Neil's hands has disappeared under the desk. My glance penetrates through piles of documents and samples of metal and glazing. I watch his hand wrap around something hanging inside the wastebasket under his desk – a weapon, judging by his attempt at surreptitiousness.

"Neil," I say patiently, "I don't have much time, but I do have within me the power to vaporize this building and reduce everything in it to little piles of dirt. Where I come from, we don't have kids anymore because we became attached to them at the expense of being kind to each other. Put your hands back on the table and use them to turn pages. Before I leave, I will explain anything you don't understand. I will make sure you can do this, and quickly. Also, insert this widget – it's an expediter – into your computer. I built it last night."

It will be a setback if it doesn't fit one of his computer's ports. Fortunately it does.

"I know it sounds like I'm a very lazy fellow (or whatever you want to call me), but I don't want a showdown with the Divider and his minions, who are within days of getting the Nobel committee to vote on – I don't mean "vote," don't make me laugh, I mean *announce* – the Nobel Prize for Physics. The recipients will be two Chinese, one Russian, and three Iranian physicists, all splitters of the gluon."

Neil is outraged. "How can you know any such thing?"

Of course what he means is, "Why not me?"

The least I can do is help Neil decipher my specs, build a prototype, and, in off hours, hang out with his kids. But Soggr's suspicion that I haven't done what I was supposed to do makes him send the lampfish, which unceremoniously vacuums me up, and we depart the planet Ocean.

Last Thoughts of the Poet
Before Dying

Dust, very fine, its shade of ochre wounding a pupil eager to capture tones and divergences: the remote distance drowning in this dust, this disintegration of stone, this sand that welcomes and warms footsteps, purposeful or desultory. Birds hurl themselves like arrows in the fullness of the late June twilight. Against the sky they impale their beaks, against the clouds they test their jaws, their shapes intimating inchoate thoughts, a multiplicity of ill-defined sensations.

All this belonged to geography and history; the assurance of being unequivocally of the present permeated every act, every idea with a peculiar magic, powerless to measure time by means of clock or calendar, rising up and transcending, being re-made in one's most complete and dazzling form.

Now we move off, and your words hurt our ears. Also, we know that you are now in the hands of the Mongols, the barbarians of the North, and that nothing is familiar to you anymore. Their eyes are not your eyes, and they sleep in tents battered by the harsh, dry wind of the steppes. What's left to you is dreams of the ramparts and the civility of your country; but those endless afternoons of plumped-up cushions are also visible to us through broken glass. This is how time passed: lingering, you sitting in the middle of musical instruments that you were too bored to play. Now you've rested. We are not closing our eyes to the golden masks buried under thirty feet of dirt, or all those stories. But because we know nothing for certain, now, only darkness and the strange death of oblivion reign. We part the shadows with our hands and want to think that everything is that easy. We don't look at the schizophrenic points of stars, their demented lights covering the sky. We don't want to hear the earth murmuring under our feet, or the crash of waves in the distance. Too many things at one time. Too much gold (and victims) in the tomb of Shub-ad, the winged bulls and the moon god Sin. What can we say about Sin? Gone, done, over. The door of Ishtar and those rampant dragons – too much! Let's focus our gaze on the room, the four cardinal points, the four seasons, the quaternary. The Sun, its design, its scorching heat. Mithras shaking the Sun's hand.

The day dawned grey, with an unsettling transparency that drew attention to the soot covering the Gothic churches, the black roofs with their empty clotheslines. A few pigeons flew around with an air of complicity. The night had seemed to me a bed of Procrustes impossible to fit into except by chopping off heads or limbs. Enter the morning, its irritating light whacking me on the forehead, that clarity of ash, that leaden gray. Feathers made of lead. I could feel the hallucinatory whirlwind of past perceptions, the attic of times of yore unleashed. The presence of the Other! Oh yes, let's begin. It's not about, no really, it isn't about filling gaps, caring about feelings, re-playing, polishing, or making splendid. Just the facts, from the observatory, from letters that come down the chimney, that crowd the attic, or better said, the observatory, coming through that telescope. "Open the doors!" the moon god shouted, and we all got angry, we all stood up and banged on the wall. Well, what else could we do? Masses of dreams, atoms, bodies, nebulae. Confusion. We heard somebody singing something. Most would say these are normal times, that we're not standing on some moving ball that whips around with no ups or downs, nothing here nor there, and all of a sudden, up pops this planet out of a top hat. There was no trick, people. The present moves quickly, the attempt to capture it as something lasting must be agile, deft, circumstantial. The desire to freeze time.

This was no trick, people. The magicians invite the public to inspect their top hats.

SONG OF THE STONE IN THE RIVER

Awareness of the blue water flowing over it, over its porous, polished surface, caused it not the least anguish as the current ran by, creating transparency and luster. And because this was so, because the water of the river ran over its face and allowed it to see when the night came and the stars moved with their almost frighteningly unexpected shafts of light – because everything was like that – phlegmatically the stone allowed itself to be carried on by the current, then felt itself overcome by a sense of joy, of jubilation. In the mornings, when the water was full of reflections and sounds as the sky grew lighter, the stone's race over the sand and moss began, following the sloping course of the channel that would eventually deposit it in a strange place where all races ended, which some called sea, and others eternity.

One afternoon, a bird with enormous strange wings, full of the colors of the rainbow, glided low over the river, filling its waters with shadows: unexpected night. Suddenly, such a chill in the heart, such harshness, night arriving with no stars or moon, a bad night for memories of the dead. The bird was flying in front of the Sun as an act of reverence because he knew he would not be flying again and that, over the racket of the forest that very night, he would have to sing his death song, a solitary call from his perch on the branch of a flowering orange tree, while the moon illuminated the river anew.

And so it happened: that very night the birdsong pierced the trees' leaves, the almost-blue newborn grasses laden with dew, the flashing eyes of animals lying awake in the dark.

When day dawned, the stone awoke to the violence of a sunbeam bearing down on its porous olive skin. During its sleep the previous night, saddened by the dying bird's cry, the stone stopped two red-and-white pebbles on their exuberant journey towards the ultimate destination. They marveled at the sight of the stone's pores and softness to the touch. Now the Sun was focusing its rays on the stone's surface; from its pores gushed steam, along with puzzlement. The Sun's radiance was too harsh, its vigor too grim, its magnificence completely self-absorbed. The waters, like crystals gathering all the light, all the blues, were running cheerfully around the stone's overheated and despondent bulk. How aloof the two white and red pebbles seemed! Silent in the face of the olive stone's sadness, they feigned not being able to hear its song of lamentation directed at the relentless Sun. At noon, when the Sun's light was at its most powerful and its strength like claws ripping through skin, the orange tree shifted one of its branches over the stone, which was sound asleep in a death-like torpor. Now the Sun could not damage the stone's core, and sometimes the wind blew through the tree's shade and birds would alight on the branch, protecting the stone. And the river, which had been growing, passed over the stone's face, giving it fresh new life.

Very soon the stone began to feel that being in the shade was causing small green plants to grow on it, and moss was covering its skin, protecting its body. It felt their roots like fine threads penetrating its pores. Its body was generous terrain for those lives that were taking nourishment from it. During long nights the vegetation grew on its calcareous skin, until the moss completely covered it, restoring its soft surface and enveloping it in a matchless green.

As yet, no one knows whether the stone, in its heart, wants to continue contentedly advancing with the fresh current of the river towards the end of those waters, which others call eternity.

A NOTE ON THE TYPE

The entire text of this book is set in Garamond, named for Claude Garamont with a "t" (1480-1561), a punch cutter who decided to work independently of printers, eventually becoming a publisher. His Roman fonts were famous for their grace and clarity, and for a century and a half they were widely emulated; he became more famous for his Greek fonts, which are still in use today. The books Garamont published were esteemed for their clear design, broad margins, fine paper, and exquisite binding. He did not die a rich man.

Acknowledgments

Heartfelt thanks to M.R. Mathews-Haney, whose eagle eyes made it possible for this book's editorial process to continue as the COVID-19 Pandemic worsened. After many technical problems related to the global situation, publication was rescheduled for May 15, 2020, in the sixth month of the COVID 19 Pandemic.

www.ingramcontent.com/pod-product-compliance
Lightning Source LLC
Chambersburg PA
CBHW032117020726
47494CB00007BA/2111

* 9 7 8 1 7 3 4 7 4 0 5 0 9 *